GHOSTBUSTERS™

Movie Novelization

Adapted by Stacia Deutsch
Based on the screenplay Written by KATIE DIPPOLD & PAUL FEIG
Based on the 1984 film "Ghostbusters" Written by DAN AYKROYD and
HAROLD RAMIS and Directed by IVAN REITMAN

Simon Spotlight
New York   London   Toronto   Sydney   New Delhi

SIMON SPOTLIGHT
An imprint of Simon & Schuster Children's Publishing Division
1230 Avenue of the Americas, New York, New York 10020
This Simon Spotlight edition June 2016
Ghostbusters TM & © 2016 Columbia Pictures Industries, Inc. All rights reserved.
All rights reserved, including the right of reproduction in whole or in part in any form.
SIMON SPOTLIGHT and colophon are registered trademarks of Simon & Schuster, Inc.
For information about special discounts for bulk purchases, please contact Simon & Schuster Special Sales at 1-866-506-1949 or business@simonandschuster.com.
Designed by Nicholas Sciacca
Manufactured in the United States of America 0516 OFF
10 9 8 7 6 5 4 3 2 1
ISBN 978-1-4814-7512-9 (pbk)
ISBN 978-1-4814-7513-6 (eBook)

PROLOGUE

"The Aldridge Mansion is the only nineteenth-century home in New York City preserved both inside and out," the tour guide said, leading his group through an old townhouse. The tourists gawked and snapped photos as he pointed toward the dining room.

He stopped in front of a thick wooden door. "Now I'm going to tell you something a little . . . spooky." All eyes focused on the guide. He lowered his voice to a whisper. "As you can see, this basement door is sealed shut." For effect, he tugged on the knob. It didn't budge.

"One morning, Sir Aldridge awoke, furious when his breakfast wasn't waiting for him. He called to his servants but none of them responded. Why?" Big pause. "Because during the night, one by one, they had each been stabbed to death in their sleep. It was later discovered they were murdered by his eldest daughter, Gertrude Aldridge." The guide knew he had captured their attention. He pointed to an oil portrait of Gertrude—she looked terrifying.

"To spare the family public humiliation, instead of turning her in to the police, Sir Aldridge locked her in the basement and fed her through this slot." He indicated a small opening in the door. "Years later when a new owner moved in, they dug out her remains. But after repeatedly hearing strange sounds emanating from the basement, he sealed it shut." The guide paused again. "That's right. No one has opened this door since. I can't imagine what Gertrude Aldridge would look like after all these years." In order to lighten the tension in the room, he added, "She wasn't looking too good before."

The group took another look at the portrait, and as he anticipated, they laughed.

Suddenly a candlestick fell off the mantle.

The group gasped. But not the guide. This candlestick was his trick, more of his show's drama. Once the group left, he'd set it back up for the next gaggle of tourists, each more gullible than the last.

 2

That night, when the tours were done and the prop candlestick was back on the mantle, the guide took one last look around before closing. Everything looked good. He grabbed his backpack and headed toward the front door when a strange rattling sound came from behind him. He looked. No one was there.

When he started out again, the rattle repeated—*ca cha, ca cha, ca cha*—causing him to turn. It was coming from the basement door. He stepped in closer to investigate.

"What . . . ?"

The knob shook as if someone or something was trying to open it. Then . . . it stopped.

BAM! Something crashed against the door.

Terrified, the tour guide bolted out of the room. The thrashing behind the door grew louder and fiercer.

Out of breath, he finally reached the front of the mansion, but the door handle refused to budge. The knob grew red hot and burned his hand. He jumped back.

Suddenly, the entire house was quiet. The guide slowly turned to discover that the sealed basement door was open.

He rushed into the living room. The candlestick he'd set up on the mantle flew at him—and this, the guide knew, was not part of his act.

He threw a nearby chair toward the window, thinking he could crawl through the glass and escape. But the chair froze midair and then flew backward, knocking him over.

He scrambled under the old dining room table and pulled the lace tablecloth down to cover himself. A moment later, the dining room table shot across the room. He looked up. Ectoplasm had begun to ooze out of the walls.

The guide was terrified. He ran through the nearest doorway and down the stairs. In shock, he realized he'd entered the basement. "Oh no . . . ," he mumbled. Slime coated the stairs, and it was now too slippery to get back up. His foot fell through one of those termite-eaten boards he'd joked about not too long ago. The entire staircase collapsed, but as he fell, he grabbed the landing and started to pull himself up. He kept pulling. . . . He was almost there. . . . He was so close . . . and that's when his face was suddenly illuminated from below.

He looked down toward the light and screamed.

 4

CHAPTER 1

Erin Gilbert was getting dressed for her day. The TV in the corner was playing a familiar song. It was the opening to a ghost-chasing reality show called *Ghost Jumpers*. Erin gave a sarcastic snort as the show's intense yet cheery host walked down the dark hallway of an abandoned mental ward.

"Who you gonna call? Ghost Jumpers!" The host introduced the program, adding, "Tonight on *Ghost Jumpers* we are locking ourselves into this abandoned mental ward for seven days straight, only allowing ourselves out to eat, sleep, and run general errands—"

Erin straightened her skirt and blouse. She checked her hair in the mirror. Once she determined that she looked respectable, she made a face at the TV.

"Uch. So stupid," Erin said, turning it off.

She opened her closet where several similar-looking plaid blazers hung in a neat row. She chose one and put it on, glancing in the mirror one last time. Yes. Respectable.

Erin grabbed her messenger bag and left the apartment.

On the front lawn of the Columbia University campus, students sat outside debating what they'd learned. Erin walked proudly through the school, nodding at a few colleagues as she passed by. She was happy. This was her dream job.

Inside Alumni Hall, members of the academic elite milled about in conversation. Erin ran a hand over the dark polished wood. She belonged here. She was respected here.

Her boyfriend, Phil Hudson, saw her come in. "Erin. Sweetheart," he said.

There was an awkward miscommunication—was Phil was going to kiss her on the lips or cheek?—but Erin was used to awkward. She brushed off the incident and allowed him to lead her across the faculty lounge.

"Did you hear?" Erin asked Phil. "I'm lecturing in the big hall today."

"Darling, that's wonderful." He took in her shirt, blouse, and jacket. "That's what you're wearing?"

 6

Erin felt a little rattled by his question. "What? Why?"

Phil shook it off. "No, you look fine. I have someone I want you to meet." A stuffy looking woman didn't smile as they approached.

"Phyllis Adler, I'd like to introduce you to Erin Gilbert. She specializes in theoretical particle physics." Phil stood between the two women. He told Erin, "Phyllis is guest lecturing in Daniel's Astrophysics and Cosmology today."

"I'm a huge fan of your work," Erin said. "It's such an honor."

Phil told Phyllis, "Erin just learned she's being published in *Nature*."

Erin beamed. "Yes, I am very proud."

Phyllis, however, shook her head. "I don't allow my lab to submit to journals anymore. I think that journals tamper with the process and ultimately hurt scientific research."

Erin struggled with how to respond. "Yes, that's true," she said, no longer smiling. "I was conflicted about the whole thing."

"It becomes more about the splash than good science," Phyllis replied. "They're completely self-serving, and the effects on science are nocuous."

Erin said, "I see what you're saying. It's like when scientists get caught up in winning some dumb award—"

Phyllis dismissed her, saying, "Oh, awards are massively important."

"Absolutely. Absolutely." Erin nodded like a bobble-head.

"It's unfortunately the only way you can draw attention to good science," Phyllis said.

"That's an excellent point." Erin checked her watch. "Well, I better get going. Lecturing in the big hall today. Give my ideas room to really spread their wings." She laughed, but Phyllis remained stone-faced.

When Erin turned to say good-bye to Phil, it was another awkward miscommunication and instead of kissing his cheek, she kissed his shoulder.

"Good luck on your tenure review!" Phil said, not seeming to notice the not-quite-a-second-kiss incident.

"Thank you. Fingers crossed," Erin said. "Not that there's anything to crossing your fingers, of course."

"I couldn't disagree more," Phyllis said. "It's been proven that superstitions can have a tremendous performance benefit."

Erin sighed. "Exactly."

After a quick walk across campus, Erin took her place at the front of a large modern lecture hall.

An older man entered the room and stopped behind her.

 8

"Aahhh!" Erin screamed when she discovered him there. Trying to regain composure, she picked up a file as if she'd been reading it all along. "Yes?"

"I'm sorry for interrupting," the man said. He introduced himself as Ed Mulgrave. "I need to speak with you about something you wrote."

Erin began to pack up her things. "All right. Which publication?"

"I'm talking about your book," he said.

Erin froze for a second, then played it off. "I'm not sure what you mean."

"You're Erin Gilbert?" He held up a thick tome and read the title. "Co-author of *Ghosts from Our Past: Both Literally and Figuratively: The Study of the Paranormal.*"

Erin continued to pack up. "I'm sorry, that must be a different Erin Gilbert."

Ed squinted at the photo inside the flap. "This really does look like you—" He turned the book toward her, then raised it next to her face.

Erin batted his hand away. "Listen, Mr. Mulgrave. That book was just sort of a joke. No self-respecting scientist really believes in the paranormal. That was a long time ago, just a gag between two friends."

Ed weighed the book in his hands. "A four-hundred-and-sixty-page gag?"

"What do you want?" Erin gave up.

"I'm the historian at the Aldridge Museum, and I believe it's haunted," Ed told her.

"Don't you give ghost tours? Isn't that the whole point?" Erin slipped her bag over her shoulder for a quick getaway.

"Yes, but that's just for fun. And ticket sales," he admitted. "But this has never happened before. It scared my tour guide nearly to death. Can you just take a look? I tried the police, but I sound crazy."

"I'm sorry, but that book you're holding is nonsense," Erin replied. "I don't know how you found it anyway. I thought I burned both copies."

"Oh, I bought it online," Ed told her. "It's on Amazon. Both hard copy and e-book."

Erin's eyes registered both shock and rage as she took in that information. She tried to hide her feelings. Very slowly she said, "Is it now?"

The instant she was alone, Erin booted up the computer in her office. She clicked on the book link.

"NO!"

 10

It was on Amazon.com. Underneath the title were two names: hers, and the other author's, Abigail L. Yates. A big picture of Erin filled the screen with the words "Ghosts are Real!" above her head in huge letters.

Erin would have exploded in anger if there hadn't been a knock at the door. It was the head of her department, Harold Filmore, coming into the small room.

"Erin—"

"What?" She quickly rotated the monitor away from him. "Yes. How is your day faring?"

"Erin . . ." Filmore was always serious. "We're set for the final review of your tenure case on Thursday, but I saw that you had a recommendation letter from Dr. Brennen at Princeton." He looked appalled. "Their science department just isn't what it used to be. I'd consider getting a referral from a more prestigious school."

Erin furrowed her brow. "More prestigious than Princ—?" She stopped herself from arguing. "Yes, of course. I can't believe I almost did that."

"I think you are an asset to modern physics and I'd hate to see you throw it down the drain." Filmore turned to leave, taking a last look at Erin before he exited. "Oh, and about your clothes."

Erin sighed. "Um . . . what about them?"

He stared at her for a moment, then said, "Never mind."

The instant he was gone, she turned back to the computer. "Abigail L. Yates," Erin read aloud, glancing at the biography. "'Abigail continues her passion for the study of paranormal at the Kenneth P. Higgins Institute of Science.'" She grunted. "Ooof."

CHAPTER 2

Erin paid her taxi driver at the entrance to the Kenneth P. Higgins Institute of Science in the Bronx and marched into the building and down the stairs to the basement. She didn't stop until she reached a door marked PARANORMAL STUDIES LABORATORY—DR. ABIGAIL YATES AND DR. JILLIAN HOLTZMANN.

A piece of paper was taped up. It read:

DO NOT WRITE STUPID THINGS ON THIS DOOR!

Erin took a dread-filled breath and knocked.

A female voice called from inside the room, "Enter!"

Erin did. The messy lab had two side offices. In the center of the room, Erin noticed some strange equipment on a long counter. And just beyond that . . . there it was. The book, on display like a trophy!

"I've been waiting a long time." The sound of that familiar voice behind her made her swell with guilt. Erin turned. She had to say something.

"Oh, Abby. That's exactly what I was afraid of—"

"I hope I got more than one wonton out of you!"

"Excuse me?" Erin looked around. Abby Yates hadn't been talking to her. She was talking to a Chinese food deliveryman.

Abby stepped forward. She was wearing a complicated antennalike piece of scientific equipment on her head. She spotted Erin and a slow fire appeared in her eyes.

"Well. My old friend Erin Gilbert . . ."

Erin wondered if maybe she shouldn't have come. The room was suddenly filled with awkward tension.

"What's on your head?" the deliveryman asked.

"An advancement in science," Abby replied, paying for her lunch and taking the bag. "That'll be all." She pointed to Erin. "And please show her the exit. I'm sure she was already looking for it."

The confused deliveryman started to show Erin to the door, but she refused to go, following Abby instead.

"Abby, we need to have a conversation," Erin said.

"I'm trying to have a conversation with the constant frequency signal I'm relaying through spectral foam. If you can be more interesting than that, be my guest," Abby said bitterly.

"You put the book online without my permission," Erin told her.

"I wasn't aware I needed your permission."

"Yes, you do, Abby. I really need you to take it down," Erin said.

"Absolutely not." Abby sat down and opened her lunch. "It's a great book. Or have you forgotten?"

"Look, I'm up for tenure right now," Erin explained. "This"— she held up the book—"comes up if you Google my name. If my colleagues see it, I will be the laughing stock of Columbia University."

Abby pulled out several food containers. "So?"

"So, there is no experimental backing for anything in that book. No one has ever been able to prove the existence of the paranormal!" Erin lowered her voice. "That book just makes us look crazy."

"Guess what? If all theories had to have experimental backing we wouldn't be anywhere! You tell Columbia University that! You give them that message from me." Abby looked down into her soup. "There is only one wonton! Unbelievable!"

Abby stormed to her office phone and hit speed-dial. "What kind of business are you running?!" she shouted into the phone. "You won't get away with this—"

Erin sat down to wait for Abby to come back. There had to be a way to convince her to take the book down! The photo on the back cover was so embarrassing. In the picture, she and Abby stood together looking very serious. They were both wearing black turtlenecks. Erin cringed at the memory.

Erin's head snapped up when she heard a woman's voice say, "You keep a lot of tension in your shoulders."

Erin hadn't noticed the woman behind the worktable, hidden behind piles of scavenged electronic components. She had her feet up and was playing with a small blowtorch. There were odd homemade weapons hanging on a pegboard behind the woman's head.

"Who are you?" Erin asked.

Abby came in from the office. "Holtzmann works with me in the lab. She's a brilliant engineer. And loyal. Would never abandon you, unlike some people I know."

"Yes, I get it." Erin was resigned to her guilt. She no longer tried to sweep it away.

Abby explained, "She specializes in experimental particle physics. She almost got hired by CERN."

"Almost?" Erin glanced at Holtzmann.

"There was a lab incident," Holtzmann said casually.

"He'll wake up." Abby was encouraging.

Holtzmann nodded. "They said he moved a finger yesterday."

"Oh, good!" Abby smiled before turning back to Erin. "She and I are bringing the ideas in our book to life. We're close on a hollow laser for the reverse tractor beam."

Erin wasn't impressed. "Terrific."

Abby didn't let her get away with the sarcasm. "It *is* terrific."

Holtzmann said to Abby, "Why don't you just let her listen to the EVP?"

"Absolutely not," Abby said.

"What EVP?" Erin was a little curious.

"Let her listen," Holtzmann told Abby. "It's the only way she'll know."

Abby groaned. "Fine. But she doesn't deserve it."

Holtzmann placed a recording device on the table. "A few months ago, we spent eight days at the Chelsea Hotel. We didn't get anything—"

"Or so we thought," Abby said. "We found this later going through the tapes."

"I should warn you," Holtzmann said just before she pressed

play. "This . . . it's upsetting what you're about to hear. It's just not from this world."

At first, Erin just heard white noise static. Holtzmann turned the volume up. The static grew louder. Erin waited, now very curious. Then . . .

FART.

Abby and Holtzmann laughed.

"Wow. Really? That's disgusting," Erin said. "Cool joke. You guys are just killing it in here."

Holtzmann smiled widely. "Oh, we have fun."

Any interest in their "science" that Erin might have had was now totally gone. "I'm so glad we could have an adult discussion about this."

"If you really don't believe in this stuff anymore, why were you looking for the book, huh?" Abby asked.

"I wasn't," Erin told her. "Some man came to see me because he thinks his building is haunted."

Abby and Holtzmann turned to each other. Then Abby asked, "What building?"

"Aldridge Mansion," Erin said.

Abby and Holtzmann quickly rushed over to a computer.

"See, that's the problem, Abby," Erin went on. "This book—this science—it encourages troubled people to indulge in their delusions. People who need *real* help, not stupid theories . . ." She looked at the two of them huddled around the computer screen. "You're not listening."

Abby and Holtzmann talked in hushed voices for a while, then Abby stood. "Let's go see some ghosts."

Without another word to Erin, they started packing strange-looking equipment into a large duffel bag.

Erin was definitely curious now, but tried to act like she wasn't.

Ready to roll, Abby reached the door and looked back at Erin. "All right, let's move."

"I'm not going on your mission," Erin said.

"Well, thank you for sending your regrets, but I didn't invite you." Abby jingled her keys. "I just can't lock this door until you're out of the room. Move it."

On the street in front of the institute, Erin watched Abby and Holtzmann hurry toward a cab. Erin felt conflicted . . . and to be honest, a little left out.

"Oh, sorry." Abby opened a cab door. "Did you want to take this cab and leave us behind? You've always been good at that."

Erin rolled her eyes and groaned.

As they loaded their equipment into the cab's trunk, Erin said, "Abby, please take down the book."

Finally, Abby agreed. "All right." But there was more. "Introduce us to this guy at Aldridge Mansion. And if we don't pick up anything there, I'll consider taking down the book until after you get your stupid tenure to your dumb university."

It was a deal. Erin climbed into the backseat of the cab. "Thank you."

20

CHAPTER 3

The tour guide at Aldridge Mansion refused to go back into the building. Erin, Abby, and Holtzmann found him outside, across the street, pacing nervously.

"Can I help you?" he asked, eyes darting left and right, as if expecting ghosts to swarm him.

"We are here to see Ed Mulgrave," Erin said. "He visited me earlier today."

"Ed Mulgrave?" the tour guide asked. "But Ed died fifteen years ago."

"Whaaaaaaaaat?" Holtzmann and Abby shrieked at the same time. Their excitement grew.

"That's ridiculous. I just saw him," Erin said.

Just then, Ed Mulgrave, the same man who visited her earlier, walked up.

"Okay . . . Who is that then?" Erin asked the guide.

"Oh, that's Ed's son, Ed Jr.," the guide answered.

"All right, that's obviously who I meant," Erin said, turning to Ed Jr.

"Thank you so much for coming," Ed Jr. said. "We've been so frightened—"

Abby cut in. "When is the last time the paranormal entity was sighted, and what on a scale of T-1 to T-5 was the level of physical interactivity?"

Ed turned to the guide. "Garret here saw it Tuesday, and I believe it made him soil himself."

The guide was embarrassed. "Really, Ed?"

Abby jumped for joy. "That's a T-3. Awesome." She was ready to start. "Let's set up inside. You can give us a tour."

"I'm not going back in there," Garret said. "Here." He tossed the keys on the ground and stepped away.

Abby, Erin, and Holtzmann entered the mansion's foyer. There was very little sunlight, making the room dark and spooky even though it was midday. While Holtzmann started filming, Abby pulled out an elaborate gadget.

"What is that?" Erin asked.

 22

"It's a PKE meter. If there's a ghost around, this baby'll let us know." Abby fiddled with a dial.

"Does it work?" Erin wondered.

"Ummm, yeah, it works," Abby said. "We just haven't seen it work because we haven't had direct contact with the paranormal." She paused. *"Yet."*

Holtzmann's camera panned the room toward Erin, who nudged it away, careful to keep out of the frame. She didn't want Columbia University to find out about this.

Abby tried to open the basement door. It wouldn't budge. "Sealed shut," she reported. "We'll come back to this. Erin, be useful and find a sledgehammer or something."

Erin threw her hands up and started exploring on her own. She discovered the terrifying portrait and shivered. Scared, she returned to Holtzmann.

"It's a fantastic book, you know," Holtzmann told her. "Nothing to be ashamed of."

Erin didn't reply as she and Holtzmann began following Abby, who was scanning everything in the room.

Abby shook her head sadly at Holtzmann and said, "Let's go check out the parlor. Too much negative energy in here." With that, Abby and Holtzmann headed through a large archway into the parlor, leaving Erin alone. She decided to just go ahead and follow them anyway, even though she'd been sort of uninvited. One step forward and her shoe slipped on something slimy.

"What is this . . . ?" Erin looked around for a drip, but then noticed that straight ahead of her the basement door was open! It had to be one of Holtzmann's ghost jokes. "Wow. Really? Again?"

Erin moved into the parlor where Abby was scanning the room with the PKE meter as Holtzmann somehow impressively both filmed and ate Pringles at the same time.

"Is there anything that isn't a joke to you guys?" Erin asked.

Abby and Holtzmann looked at each other, confused.

"You didn't open the basement door?" Erin hesitated.

Abby was clearly shocked at the news. "The basement door is open?" She looked for herself and was surprised to find Erin was telling the truth.

"Well if it wasn't you, it's probably just Ed or th—" Erin's voice stilled as she looked out the window to where Ed and the tour guide were still on the sidewalk.

Abby's PKE meter lit up and the antenna began to spin. "I didn't even know it did that!" she said.

Creeeaaakkk. It sounded like a footstep on the basement stairs. *Creeeaaakkk.* Then another one.

 24

"My ears just popped. Definite AP-XH shift. I don't think we're alone."

Abby grabbed the camera from Holtzmann, and dim colored light began to glow from inside the stairwell.

"Please tell me you're seeing that," Abby gasped.

They were. A ghost floated toward them. She was none other than Gertrude Aldridge.

Abby lowered the camera to take a closer look. "It's a class four, distinct human form apparition."

"This isn't happening," Erin muttered.

"Oh, it's happening all right," Holtzmann assured her.

"And it's the most beautiful thing I've seen." Abby's eyes were wide.

Slowly, Erin took a step toward it. "It can't be real. . . ." She reached out her hand.

"Careful!" Abby warned. "It could be malevolent. We've never made contact before."

Erin felt safe. "No. She looks peaceful somehow."

She turned to the ghost. "Hello, ma'am. My name is Erin Gil—"

But Gertrude Aldridge was not peaceful. She tipped her head down. Suddenly, she looked malicious. She opened her mouth and ectoplasm shot out in a mighty spray, covering Erin and blasting her back.

"Get down!" Abby screamed.

They all dropped to ground as the ghost darted through the wall and left the mansion.

Erin, Abby, and Holtzmann ran out of the building just in time to see Gertrude Aldridge fly down the street.

Erin was in shock. "What just happened?"

"What just happened?" Abby grabbed Erin and shook her. "We saw a ghost!"

Erin processed that. "We did! We saw a ghost!"

Together, the three women jumped up and down, hugging each other excitedly.

"Ghosts are real," Erin said as Abby recorded her.

CHAPTER 4

At Columbia University, Erin sat across from Harold Filmore in his office. He turned the computer screen toward her so she could get a closer look at the video he was watching.

It was of Erin, standing outside Aldridge Mansion. She was dancing with Abby and Holtzmann and cheering, "Ghosts are real! Ghosts are real!"

Dr. Filmore paused the video. "Dr. Bronstein saw this on Reddit. It was reblogged from a Dr. Abigail Yates's site, Ghost News. I hadn't heard of that publication."

Erin raised her hands in protest. "Wait—you don't think that's me in the video, do you?"

Filmore simply stared at her. The video was paused on Erin's face.

"But this isn't something I'm really involved with. Truly." She felt panicked. This couldn't be happening! Not now!

"I hope you understand that when we give people tenure, they represent this institution," Filmore said. "They affect such things as grants and our standing in the collegiate rankings."

Erin's face fell. Then she forced a smile, awkwardly leaning back in her chair. She clasped her hands into finger guns. "Gotcha. Ha! You should've seen your face."

"Please don't pretend this is a prank," Filmore said.

Erin dropped her fingers and frowned. "Okay."

"I'm sorry. This just isn't what this institution is about." Filmore closed down the video.

"It's not what I'm about either! I'm about real, serious science." Erin had a new approach to this crisis. "That's why I conducted this test, so congratulations, Dr. Filmore—" She reached out to shake his hand.

But Filmore wasn't buying it. "This is just uncomfortable now," he told her.

Next plan—escape. "Well, my class starts in an hour, so I'd better get back to it." Erin stood.

Harold Filmore stared at her. And that's when Erin knew.

Class was canceled. Erin was fired.

//////////////////////

28

Erin kicked open the door to the paranormal lab at the Kenneth P. Higgins Institute. Abby and Holtzmann were watching TV. They looked up, surprised to see her.

"Well, I hope you're happy." Erin grabbed a piece of equipment from the lab to throw across the room.

Abby and Holtzmann shouted together, "Nooooo! We'll all die!"

Erin put the thingy back down carefully, then grabbed an ammeter to throw.

"Nooooo! We only have one of those!" Abby stopped her.

Erin put it down. "How could you do that? How could you put that online? I was fired. Everyone was watching. I was completely humiliated!"

"All right, knock it off," Abby said. "Now, I'm sorry, but we saw a real ghost. How long have we been looking for that? And she was beautiful, Erin." Abby reconsidered. "Well, until she dislocated her jaw and ecto-projected all over you. But even that was beautiful."

Erin thought about it, relenting ever-so-slightly. "There was a heavy ionization discharge. I could smell it. Somehow it got energized."

"Full-torso transmogrification with corporeal aggression. Right before our eyes!" Abby was up and pacing. "And we're

29

supposed to be quiet about it? We've been working our whole lives for this. And we got almost a hundred comments. Not just crazies. Read this one."

Abby pointed. "This lady describes a class three haunting in her home. She's scared. She lives alone and can't afford to move. We can provide a real service here. She can't call the police. She can't call a friend. Who is she going to call?"

As if it was meant to be, the *Ghost Jumpers* theme song started up on the television and the announcer shouted, "Ghost Jumpers!"

Abby searched for the remote. "These phonies. They make it harder for people like us! This can't be the only option to the people. We're on the cusp of discovery here. And I know you love being on the cusp."

"I do, I love the cusp," Erin nodded, feeling teary.

"Now, I know this isn't Columbia. But the Kenneth P. Higgins Institute—" Abby began.

"Ughhhhhh," Erin grunted.

"That's *insanely* rude, but I'll ignore it—the Higgins Institute grants us money and they let us study whatever we want. They don't even ask what we're doing. We have been left alone for almost a year. Watch. I'll go ask them for more funding right now." Abby lead Holtzmann and

 30

Erin out of the lab and to the administration offices.

They got right in to see the dean.

"I honestly just didn't know your department still existed. I can't believe this has gone on this long," the dean said.

"What?" Abby cried.

The dean explained. "I'm sorry, but ghosts? No, no, no. We simply cannot let the twelve year history of this institution be smeared by this."

"Oh, come on," Abby said. "Suddenly this school has a classy reputation to uphold?" She pointed under the desk. "You're wearing shorts."

It wasn't just Erin anymore. Now they'd *all* been fired.

As Holtzmann and Abby pushed their heavy equipment out of the basement, Erin had a plan. "You know what? We're going to show everyone we're not crazy. We just have to capture an entity and bring it into a controlled environment."

Abby was realistic. "We have no lab. We also have no money."

Erin said, "I have some savings. Do either of you have any savings?"

"I was planning on asking if I could borrow some," Holtzmann replied.

Erin found herself growing more and more optimistic. "We

can do this. We're gonna be the first scientists to ever prove the paranormal exists."

Abby smiled. "That's the Erin I used to know. Welcome back. Now, let's get out of here with this stuff before they make us give it back."

Behind them, the door to the college flung open.

"Hey, bring that back here!" the dean shouted.

They got away.

 32

CHAPTER 5

Patty Tolan worked at a subway station. Sometimes she felt really lonely, sitting all by herself at the ticket window. Patty was feeling particularly lonely when a few passengers hurried past on their way to the platform.

"How are you guys doing?" Patty called out to them. A woman in a blue shirt speed-walked past her. "I have that same shirt," Patty continued. The woman still didn't listen. "Except mine is purple and long-sleeve. You know what? It's just a different shirt."

The woman boarded a train and was gone. "Get home safe," Patty said with a long sigh. She accepted that the rest of her shift would be lonely.

Just as she accepted this, Patty jumped. There was a man by the booth, staring at her!

It was Rowan, the maintenance man from the Mercado Hotel.

"They will always ignore you. They are walking sewage, focused only on their own trivial matters," said Rowan.

Patty was used to people talking nonsense in the train station. "Uh-huh. Everything good?" she said.

"Take pride in your work," Rowan replied, his voice distant and monotone.

Patty glanced around the ticket booth. "Well, I don't know about that. Can I help you with something?"

Rowan leaned in toward her. "When the Fourth Cataclysm begins, the laborers will be among the last led to the butchery. So make the most of your extra time."

Patty gave a small shrug. "Oh, okay, my man. Thanks so much. Have a great day."

Rowan nodded as if he'd passed important information, then walked away.

Patty shrugged and went back to reading her book.

The next time she glanced up, Rowan was on her security monitor. He was climbing down off the train platform and into a train tunnel.

 34

Patty grabbed her flashlight. "Oh, come on," she muttered.

She hurried to where she'd last seen him, but he was gone. She looked toward the end of the platform. No sign of Rowan. Before she went back to the booth, a weird flash of light appeared deep in the tunnel. Patty shone her flashlight in. "Hello?" she called out. No response. She had no choice but to check it out.

Deeper inside the subway tunnel, she found something attached to the wall. It was a strange homemade box, shooting off sparks like mini-fireworks. A ghostly wave of energy flowed from it.

"What . . . ?" Patty leaned in for a better look. It was then she noticed something else . . . a creepy, tall, thin glowing man was walking deeper into the tunnel! He wore an old striped prison uniform and had a metal cap on his head.

Patty didn't notice Rowan watching the tall man from the shadows.

The sparking device next to her burst into flames and fell apart. Patty jumped back, but wasn't hurt. She called after the tall man, "Hey! You can't go down there."

The man stopped. That was when Patty noticed his feet were several inches off the ground. He was a ghost!

Patty was sufficiently creeped out. "Go wherever you want,"

she said, now that she knew he wasn't alive. "They don't pay me enough for this." She dropped her flashlight on the tracks and ran away.

Meanwhile, Erin, Abby, and Holtzmann moved into their new headquarters. It was an old dining room on the second floor of a rundown Chinese restaurant. Abby and Holtzmann's equipment filled every available spot.

Abby stood at the door talking to the deliveryman. "How does it take you an hour to walk up a flight of stairs? I move above you, and you still can't help me out?" She pulled her soup out of the bag and opened it. "This is just broth and one shrimp. That's not soup, that's a pet."

While Abby argued over her lunch, Erin watched Holtzmann working in the space that she'd claimed as her lab. She was wearing a hazmat suit, testing sensitive equipment while dancing to the music on the radio. When she accidentally lit a paper towel dispenser on fire, Holtzmann danced over to the extinguisher and grooved back to put out the fire with a fancy disco spin.

After things had calmed down, there was a knock at the door.

A man entered. "Excuse me. I'm here about the receptionist job?"

Erin stared at the man. He was incredibly handsome.

When she didn't speak, he said, "Hello?"

Erin blinked hard and said, "Of course. Let's go into the conference room."

"Are you Kevin?" asked Abby. "Fantastic! We spoke on the phone, follow me!"

The elegant and iconic Mercado Hotel was known for many things, mostly its proximity to Times Square. What it was not known for, however, was a small cluttered apartment in the basement maintenance room. That room belonged to a man named Rowan. In the room, a sad cot sat in the corner. Above it, on the walls, were framed physics diplomas from Stanford and MIT.

"You will do a great job today," Rowan North told himself as he buttoned his uniform for work. "Your potential is matched only by your ambition. Trust in your abilities and the universe shall bend before your will."

A voice boomed through a speaker on the wall. "Rowan, we've got a clogged toilet on 1843. It's bad. Get on it ASAP."

"Absolutely. Nothing would make me happier," Rowan replied. It didn't matter that he was dripping sarcasm. The voice didn't care.

37

Before leaving, Rowan took a quick glance into his mirror and grinned at the dark otherworldly shadows lurking behind the glass.

"And the universe shall bend before your will," he repeated.

Meanwhile, back at headquarters, the Ghostbusters and Kevin entered the conference room, which was really just a booth at the restaurant.

Abby opened a notebook filled with questions. "First off, congratulations. To walk through this door already tells me that you have a daring and curious mind."

Kevin tipped his head. "Sure."

"Everyone here has an unyielding passion to answer the unanswered questions. A life-long dedication." She glanced at Erin. "Well, most of us. She's in and out. But for the most part, everyone here is fiercely dedicated—"

Erin cut in. "Okay, he doesn't need our history." Abby shrugged. Erin said, "So, you must be curious about what we do."

"Definitely. Do you work Wednesdays?" Kevin asked.

"Uh, yes. Yes, we work Wednesdays," Erin said.

"Shoot. That's tough for me," Kevin said.

"Well, let's get to it." Abby tapped her pencil on the table. "Big question. Do you believe in ghosts?"

 38

"Um. Not really," Kevin responded.

"Oh? Oh." Abby looked disappointed, and then flipped through her notebook. "All these follow-up questions were based on a yes." She slowly closed her notebook.

Kevin reconsidered his answer. "You mean like Casper?"

Abby got excited. "Yes! Like Casper. Okay. He gets it."

Erin frowned. "Does he, though?"

"Kevin also dabbles in web design, so I asked him to try a couple logos out for us. Show us what you've got," Abby said.

Kevin opened his laptop. The first logo was a drawing of a silly looking cartoon ghost.

Abby tried to make the best of it. "Well, look at all that effort. Sometimes it's not about the end product but the journey."

"Kevin, you do see how that makes us look bad, right?" Erin asked him.

Kevin nodded, but Erin thought he might also be clueless.

Kevin pulled out another logo. This one was a hot dog floating over a house.

"Is that supposed to be for us?" Erin asked.

Kevin looked at Abby. "She said on the phone 'a ghost or miscellaneous.'"

"Oh, no, actually I said a 'ghost, but nothing extraneous.'"

Abby added, "Okay, so just a misunderstanding."

Holtzmann was still looking at the hot dog logo. "I still have so many questions about this choice."

Erin rose from the table. "Um, Kevin, could you excuse us for a moment?"

When Kevin was gone, Erin said, "We can't do this. We are scientists. We are trying to do something real."

"He's the only applicant." Abby glanced over at Kevin.

"Really?" Erin followed Abby's gaze. Across the room, Kevin was acting odd.

"Erin, he chose us. That means something. And we of all people should know better than to judge others," Abby said. "We don't know what's in there. I see a natural curiosity in him."

Erin figured out what Kevin was up to. "He's trying to get the phone through the glass."

There was a fish tank left over from the restaurant. Inside was an old broken phone. Kevin was repeatedly bumping his hand against the empty aquarium's glass trying to get at it.

"How am I supposed to answer the phone in there?" he asked.

Abby ignored him. "Look, Erin. Everyone has something to offer. You walk into this laboratory/Chinese restaurant and

 40

you will be welcome. I'm telling you, there's something in there."

Kevin found an old gong and hit it.

Abby shouted over to Kevin. "You got the job!"

Erin made a face, but noticed Kevin looking at her. She gave him a thumbs-up and a forced smile. "Welcome aboard!"

"Cool. Can I bring my suitcases up?" Kevin asked.

"Yes, you may," Abby said.

As Kevin headed out the door, Abby noticed a woman sitting at the top of the stairwell, reading a magazine. "Ma'am, if you're picking up takeout, wait downstairs," Abby said.

"Oh. I saw this magazine and thought this was your waiting room," the woman said. Abby didn't know it yet, but this was Patty. She put the magazine on the floor and came inside. Patty knew a lot about the history of the building where the Ghostbusters had their headquarters, but that wasn't why she was there. "I was just chased by a ghost," she told them.

CHAPTER 6

Patty led Erin, Abby, and Holtzmann into the subway and down the tunnel where she'd seen the ghost. Abby used the PKE meter while Holtzmann pushed a large, clunky proton box on wheels.

"You know, the old York Prison used to be right there above us," Patty said. "I always knew there was something weird down here."

Abby checked her meter. "Strong correlation between negative incidents and paranormal presence. It's very difficult for anything to pass through the barrier back into our world." Abby twisted a few dials, then went on. "So any spirit determined enough to pull that off, well, that's likely an angry ghost."

Patty noticed a graffiti artist ahead. "Hey! What did I say?!"

He pretended to spray his armpits.

"That is not deodorant! Have you again mistaken me for a stupid person?" Patty shook a fist at him.

"Is he down here a lot?" Abby asked.

"This is his art studio," she said.

Abby called to the artist, "Have you seen a class four semi-anchored entity around here?"

Patty whispered, "You might want to try English."

Erin asked, "Have you seen a ghost?"

The graffiti artist replied, "Yeah, I've seen a ghost."

"Can you describe it?" Erin asked.

The graffiti artist thought about it for a minute, then started to draw an outline of a ghost on the subway wall.

"Don't you draw a ghost on that wall," Patty warned.

He stopped. Then he spray-painted a little more.

"I mean it." Patty said as he put the finishing touches on his art. "I don't want that ghost up there."

He drew a circle with a line through it over the ghost.

Patty ran forward and grabbed the spray paint from his hand. The artist ran away, and Patty fumed. Meanwhile Holtzmann peeked back at the graffiti on the wall. What remained was a spray-painted outline of a ghost in a red circle with a line through it.

Holtzmann snapped a shot of the artist's image with her phone, and then ran to catch the others, who had left to find the ghost farther down.

Abby used her PKE meter and EMF meter.

"We don't have much time," Patty told them. "No one touch the third rail."

A drip of green slime fell from the ceiling onto Erin's shoulder. "Oh, come on. I just dry-cleaned this," she said.

"Yeah, I figured you were gonna get your fancy clothes dirty down here. I should have given you some coveralls. My bad," Patty said.

Abby called them all together. "We got something going on over here. Is that a burn mark?"

"That's where I saw that weird sparking thing." Patty pointed at the wall where the strange box had been mounted.

"What was it?" Holtzmann asked.

"Darlin', if I knew, I wouldn't have said 'that weird sparking thing.'"

Abby began collecting samples from around the area. She found a large a chunk of debris. "Smells of both electrical discharge and isotopic decay." She handed it over to Holtzmann. "Holtz, smell this. You agree?"

Holtzmann smelled it, then licked it. "Definite neutron burn."

 44

Patty was repulsed. "All right, if you're all done kissing that piece of dirty garbage, we only have a few minutes. For real. I gave us no cushion room."

Just then, the lights in the tunnel flickered and went out.

Holtzmann pointed down the tunnel. "Do you see that? The eyes."

Erin sighed. Another prank? "Holtzmann, please don't mess—oh—" There was something down there in the dark. It looked like a pair of glowing yellow eyes. "That is unsettling."

"Holtzmann, illuminate the subject," Abby ordered.

"Yeah, get some light on that," Patty agreed while getting ready to run.

Holtzmann shone the flashlight down the tunnel, revealing the ghost. He was the tall, thin, pale prisoner-ghost Patty had seen before. His yellow eyes flashed at them.

The PKE meter's antenna started spinning wildly.

Erin noted the meter. "That is somehow more unsettling."

"And fantastic! That's another class four, but way more ionized than the Aldridge ghost. Look at the meter. I've gotta get this on film." Abby grabbed the camera. "Let's bring this boy to the lab. Holtz, power up." Abby started filming.

"This is early stages, so it's a little rough. I'm going to adjust the levels. Erin, hold this." Holtzmann handed Erin a large, cumbersome wand. It was attached to a tube that attached to a box. "This will shoot a proton stream, so just aim it at the ghost when I say. Oh, I almost forgot." She put a contraption that looked like a metal neck brace around Erin's neck and connected it with a wire to the machine. "Just a little bit of grounding." Holtzmann confirmed that Erin was ready. "Okay, don't move too much. Or talk. And definitely don't sweat."

Erin stood frozen like a robot while Holtzmann fiddled with switches on the proton box.

"Holtzmann," Erin muttered between closed lips. The ghost was getting closer.

"Aim the wand at it," Abby told Erin. She did, but only a weak beam shot out. "Well, that's underwhelming. Use more power."

Holtzmann adjusted the settings. "Okay, Erin, do it again."

She aimed the wand again and the beam went a little farther. It touched the ghost, but just barely.

Erin was dripping sweat. "Can this get stronger please?!"

Holtzmann tried a few things. "Not at the moment. Live and learn, I guess. I wish I had time to run back to the lab." She asked Erin, "You couldn't hold that for a while, could you?"

"NO!" The beam from Erin's wand was holding the ghost, who was now only two feet in front of her.

 46

"Think you could just slowly drag it back to the lab like this?" Holtzmann suggested.

"NO!"

The ghost suddenly pushed forward against the beam. Erin fell backward onto the tunnel floor, but managed to hold on.

Lights in the distance made Patty shriek. "That's the train. We gotta move!"

"We are not losing this thing," Abby said. "Erin, drag the ghost back to the platform."

"What?" Erin could barely speak.

"There's no time! Grab her sides!" Patty took hold of the back of Erin's collar like a kitten and lifted her as Holtzmann and Abby helped.

The train got closer.

"That's express! It's not stopping!" Patty warned.

They pulled Erin up to the platform just in time. But the proton box was still on the track. Holtzmann ripped the attached metal collar off Erin's neck seconds before the train's impact slammed the box into the third rail, causing electricity to surge up through the tube. The ghost was captured for a second, until a surge of electricity hit him, sending ectoplasm splattering. Erin was covered.

Abby and Holtzmann glanced up in time to see the ghost in

47

the back of the subway car, looking confused as it sped away.

"Guess he's going to Queens," Patty said calmly.

"Did you see that?" Abby nearly screamed. "That surge of power really got a hold of it. What a field test! Data-tastic!"

Holtzmann was taking notes. "Yep. We're going to need a lot more juice. We need to be more mobile, too. I know what to do."

"We almost got killed," Erin choked out. She was covered in ectoplasm.

"Yeah, I know," Holtzmann was thrilled. "So awesome. No one looked into that flash, right?"

Erin gasped. "I looked directly into it."

"Oh, that's fine," Holtzmann said.

But she made a face at Abby and mouthed, "Yikes."

CHAPTER 7

Back at headquarters, Erin watched the subway video that
Abby had posted. All the comments were pretty much the
same. "Fake." "You people are crazy."

Erin couldn't believe it. "What do people want?" She turned
to Abby. "We really need to get a ghost back to the lab and
document it properly. This stuff's all real and we can't prove
it to anybody."

"We will." Abby was confident. "You just gotta ignore these
people."

Kevin brought Abby a cup of coffee.

"Did you remember the sugar?" she asked.

Kevin wasn't sure, so he took a long sip, then gave the cup
to Abby. "Yeah." He walked away.

"Well, at least he remembered," Abby said, setting the cup aside.

"What do you make of the tech from the subway?" Erin asked as they studied the leftover parts from the sparking device on a table.

"I've only got bits and pieces here, none of which have any business in a subway tunnel. But look at this—" Abby held up a piece.

"Was that a miniature cyclotron?" Erin asked.

"Yup," Abby confirmed. "Everything I'm looking at here, they're all things we've associated with attracting ghost particles. I'm wondering if someone built some kind of device to bring in an apparition. Which is very impressive."

Erin glanced at Patty, who was sitting at a computer in the office, typing madly. "What was that weird thing that guy mentioned?"

"The Fourth Cataclysm," Patty replied. "Sounded like some spooky ancient stuff. But I can't find anything about it online." She shook her head. "Do I need to worry about first through third cataclysms? Who's got that kind of time?"

Abby and Erin looked at each other, then back at Patty.

"Ma'am, why are you still here?" Erin asked.

 50

"Oh, I'm joining your club," Patty said, as if it was totally obvious.

The phone rang. Kevin looked at Erin before answering. "What is this place called again?"

"Conductors of the Metaphysical Examination," Erin said, proud of the name.

Kevin answered the phone. "Conductors of Meta Something or Other."

"Hey, Kevin?" Abby interrupted. "I'm going to need you to try a little harder, okay, buddy?"

Kevin put down the receiver. "Okay, if they call back I will."

Abby smiled. "There you go."

"I gotta take off, though. I've got a hide-and-seek tournament. We're in the semis." Kevin started gathering his stuff.

Abby didn't have to look at Erin to know her face was disapproving.

Erin turned back to Patty. "Patty, this isn't really a club. We're a research group. Do you have any lab experience?"

"No. And I kind of feel like I was set up to fail with that question. No, I am not a scientist, I understand that." Patty went on, "I didn't go to some fancy school like the rest of you. But I read a lot of nonfiction. You know, you can be smart about science but a straight up dummy about everything else."

51

She calmed down. "I guess I didn't need to insult you. I apologize for that." She took a breath. "Look, I spend most of my time sitting alone in an MTA booth. Thought it would be nice to pick up an activity that involves other people." She added, "Also I could borrow a car from my uncle so you don't have to keep lugging all that heavy equipment around."

That last point they couldn't refuse.

"Great. Welcome to the team, Patty," Abby said for them all.

The next morning there was a loud honking on the street in front of the restaurant. Abby, Erin, and Holtzmann came out the front door to find Patty getting out of her uncle's hearse.

"Oh, sweet!" Holtzmann cheered.

"You did not disclose this automobile was a hearse," Abby said, circling Patty and the car.

Patty was insulted. "My uncle owns a funeral home. Would you rather take the subway? What's the difference? We work with the dead anyway."

Meanwhile, Rowan walked down the narrow hallways of the Mercado, swinging an electric device in his hands. A door at the end of the hall opened and an older woman, Mrs. Potter, stood there in a bathrobe.

 52

"Excuse me! Maintenance man," Mrs. Potter called out.

"Mrs. Potter! Thank you for using my preferred title," Rowan said, dripping sarcasm. "How may I help you?"

"Well, for starters you could tell me what this is." She pointed to the doorframe, where green slime was oozing down the wall.

"Isn't that something? Must be leakage from the air conditioning," Rowan said with a small grin. "I'll take care of it immediately."

"I think it must have touched my skin. It's given me a rash." She pulled up the back of her blouse and showed her back to Rowan. "Does this look red to you?"

Rowan discovered that a small ghostly creature was living inside Mrs. Potter. It gnashed its teeth and tried to claw its way out through her back.

"Well." He took a closer look, then told her, calmly, "I was gonna say no, but you know what? Yep. It's a little red . . . right in this area here. Does it look bad? No, not at all. But just in case, I'll send up some cream."

His smile turned sinister as he walked quickly down to the basement.

Once alone, Rowan took off his jacket and hung it carefully behind the door. Before getting to work, Rowan looked into the large mirror reflecting the ghost world, and said, "I know everyone is anxious, but we must be patient. The guests are starting to complain. We don't want any spoilers before the big show."

CHAPTER 8

It was dinnertime. Erin, Abby, Patty, and Holtzmann were hanging out, eating pizza.

"So, how did you two meet?" Patty asked Abby and Erin.

"Abby transferred to my high school junior year," Erin answered.

Abby continued, "We started sharing ghost stories and bonded immediately. All the other kids were going to parties, and we were like, 'that's stupid.'"

"Also, we weren't invited to any parties," Erin said.

"Well, we also put out a vibe that indicated we were not accepting any invitations," Abby put in.

Erin shook her head and muttered, "Not really."

That was all good, but Patty wanted to know more. "Why were you so into ghosts? Had either one of you actually seen one?"

Erin stiffened. Abby was quiet.

At last, Erin said, "Yeah. When I was eight, the mean old lady who lived next door to us died. That night I woke up, and there she was, standing at the foot of my bed. She was just staring at me, and then blood started coming out of her mouth. She started slowly falling toward me. I pulled my covers over my head and waited until morning."

Patty was about to comment, when Erin added, "She did that every night for a year."

"What?" was all Patty could say.

"Whoa," uttered Holtzmann.

"I told everyone, but no one believed me. My parents thought I was crazy. They had me in therapy for years. All the kids at school made fun of me. Called me 'ghost girl.' But Abby believed me right away."

"Hey. I believe you too," Patty said.

Holtzmann wasn't so fast. "Hmm, I have some questions." Then, she winked and Erin laughed.

"You know, I never connected with the other kids either. Mostly because I was into books. I think my experience was perhaps less traumatic than yours," Patty said as Kevin walked in, casually playing with something in his hands.

"Erin, if you don't believe in yourself," he said, "no one else will."

Erin was surprised by his compassion. "Thank you. That's really nice."

Suddenly, Abby looked alarmed. "Kevin, what's in your hand?"

He opened his palm to reveal the same the piece of equipment that Erin had picked up back at Higgins. If Kevin dropped it, they'd all die.

"What? This?" Kevin joked around, juggling the strange looking thing.

"Kevin, no!" Holtzmann shrieked.

"Do not let it fall!" Abby said in a tone that told him she was serious.

Kevin juggled the thing like it was a hot potato.

Holtzmann said slowly, very slowly, "Just stop juggling and put it down!"

He did . . . and they all took a breath.

As the tension settled, Patty picked up a photo on the desk. "Hey, what's this?" The image was of two awkward teenagers, Erin and Abby, looking geeky and happy.

"Science fair!" Erin immediately recognized the shot.

"I found it this morning," Abby said.

Patty read the title on the poster in the picture. "'The Durable But Not Impenetrable Barrier!' What does that mean?"

"Oh, I wish we still had the presentation. It was fantastic," Erin said, then she noticed a smirk behind Abby's eyes.

"That wish might just be granted . . . ," Abby said.

Erin looked at Abby with wide eyes. "You still have it?"

Abby brought out the poster board from the science fair presentation! It was covered with ghostly illustrations.

Abby and Erin stood in front of the board. They looked very serious. They began acting out their routine.

"Good evening," they said together.

Patty looked to see how far the door was and considered making a quick getaway, but Holtzmann stopped her. "I've only heard about this. Never actually seen it. This is history."

Abby and Erin announced in unison, "Prepare for takeoff into the unknown in five . . . four . . . three . . . two . . . one."

Abby pressed play on an old tape recorder, and spooky music began to play. Then they acted like planets. Abby rotated around Erin.

"The universe is mysterious," Erin said.

"Ninety-six percent mysterious," Abby added.

"And what of the topic of ghosts?" Erin asked.

Abby whispered, "They're real!" Music boomed and they danced.

"Then why don't I see ghosts flying everywhere?!" Erin asked.

"The barrier stops them," Abby explained. "It is the only line of defense in the portal between the worlds of the living and the dead."

"Now, let's break it down," Abby said.

The music turned to an old-school hip-hop beat.

Erin started rapping. "Yo. How many different types of ghosts we got, A?"

Abby rapped back. "Humanoids, vapors . . ."

Patty was glaring at Abby and Erin.

"You know what, let's skip ahead," Abby said.

"Yeah, that part is thirty minutes long and involves break dancing," Erin said.

The break dancing was actually pretty good, but they skipped it and started the act again when Abby and Erin announced, "So protect the barrier! Protect the barrier! Or mankind will end." It ended with Abby and Erin striking rapper poses. "Word!"

Abby and Erin laughed, hugging and celebrating. "We remembered it!"

Holtzmann joined them in the hugs. "I am so happy you two are together again. So happy," she said.

Erin and Abby then looked at Patty.

"I was all set to make fun of you, but that was actually beautiful," Patty admitted. "It was good you had each other."

Erin and Abby simply smiled. Over their shoulders, Holtzmann noticed something on the muted television. "Hey, look." She turned up the volume just as the NYC reporter was saying, "—a local team of paranormal investigators released a video of a proclaimed ghost—"

It was their footage. Erin was clearly visible.

Patty moved to a better spot to see. "We're famous!"

The newscaster said, "So, what do we think of these 'Ghostbusters'?"

"Ghostbusters? They can't make up a name for us, can they?" Erin asked.

"No, she just misspoke—" Abby started, but just then it flashed across the screen: *Discussing the Ghostbusters*.

"Oh." Abby realized she was wrong.

The reporter said, "I spoke with Martin Heiss earlier, of the Council for Logic and Data, *and* famed debunker of the paranormal."

"Tell me. Is this for real?" the reporter asked Mr. Heiss.

"No," Heiss said.

"Thank you." The reporter faced the camera, "Coming up, Mayor Bradley on the rolling blackouts."

"Unbelievable. Do you know that we only know what four percent of the universe is? How quick they are to say no!" Abby exclaimed.

"Oh man. Now *we're* the ghost girls." Patty turned to Erin. "I suddenly feel your pain."

Erin turned off the news just as the phone started ringing in the background.

"We are scientists, and we rely on controlled tests and provable physical results," Erin said, feeling determined. "And so, we are going to catch a ghost and bring it back to this lab. And Kevin . . ." The phone was still ringing. "Answer the phone!"

Kevin put down the pictures he was looking at and answered, "Conductor something."

They all looked at him, waiting to hear what the call was about.

"Uh-huh. Cool, thanks, bye." Kevin hung up. He went back to comparing two different headshot options. He held up the photos. "Hey, which of these makes me look more like a doctor?"

"Whichever one tells us who was on the phone!" Erin said through clenched teeth.

"Someone from the Stonebrook Theatre," Kevin said. "I don't know . . . something's happening there."

"Yes!" Erin punched air.

"I'll get the car," Holtzmann said.

They all got ready to go. Abby told Kevin, "All right, when I get back we're gonna start off with parallel universes and entanglement." Lessons were necessary.

"What?" Kevin looked blank.

Abby grinned. "He's curious already!"

They were leaving to go to the Stonebrook Theatre, when Patty handed Erin an armload of subway uniforms. "I took these from work and made 'em look all official. Put 'em on if you don't want to get slimed again."

CHAPTER 9

Patty's uncle's hearse, now called Ecto-1, raced through the streets of Manhattan. Holtzmann didn't slow until they pulled up outside the theater. A few concert-goers were hanging around outside. The Ghostbusters got out of the car, wearing their subway uniforms and proton packs, ready for action.

Inside, the concert was in full swing. Heavy metal music fans milled around at the concessions and in the lobby, while others danced near the stage.

Jonathan, the manager, rushed over. "Are you the Ghostbusters?"

"Yes, we are," Abby said.

"But I was told a 'Doctor' Yates was coming," Jonathan said.

Insulted, the Ghostbusters turned around to leave.

"Whoa, wait, wait! It's not because you're women. It's because you're dressed like garbage men." Jonathan had to step aside as the paramedics wheeled a theater janitor past on a gurney. He was muttering, "I have looked into the eyes of the demon. I have looked into the eyes of the demon. . . ."

The girls watched him go by, then Jonathan said, "Follow me. Please."

He led the Ghostbusters down some stairs and through a series of hallways under the theater. Adam, a lead singer for the next band up, was backstage arguing with Eugene, the bass player, and Ely, the drummer.

"I saw you look at him when I was talking, like what I was saying was stupid." Eugene was in Adam's face.

"Don't do this now. I have sunk every last penny into a ton of effects for this show, and we've got the head of Thunder Gun Records out there scouting us! Now let's go." Adam ended the fight by shoving Eugene up the stairs. Ely followed. The Ghostbusters passed them by.

"Fernando was down here when something came out of the wall vent and attacked him. I heard his screams and when I came to see, some 'thing' was throwing him all over the place," Jonathan explained.

Abby looked to Erin. "A T-5 interaction?"

"Great. This is great," Erin said.

"Not for Fernando," Jonathan replied. "I thought it was going to kill him. I shrieked when I saw it, and I guess I scared it because it flew off down the hall. I'm told my scream is quite disturbing." He stopped as they reached the hall of an old wing. His face reflected the horror he'd seen. "Whatever is down there, I hope I'll never come across it again. It will haunt me every night when I go to sleep. No one should ever have to encounter that kind of evil." He pointed the way. "Anyway, keep walking that way and you'll find it."

"Oh good," Patty said.

"We'll get it. Don't worry." Erin was confident.

"One thing we might need from you, Jonathan, is some . . ." Abby turned to him, then pinched her lips and said, "Oh, he's already taken off? Okay."

The hallway divided into several directions.

Abby was on it. "All right, it could be anywhere. Let's split up." She tapped the walkie-talkie on her belt. "Walkie if you see anything."

A few moments later, Erin passed a wardrobe displaying fake heads wearing wigs. Holtzmann was going down another way, wearing one of the wigs.

65

Erin raised her proton wand. "Holtzmann! This is serious!"

"And I agree." Holtzmann flipped her hair back and grinned.

Patty walked down a dark backstage hall. She was on edge, aiming her proton pack at everything.

She muttered to herself as she went. "I thought this was going to be like a book club. You know, have a snack, talk about ghosts, that sort of thing."

She peeked into a room filled with mannequins. "Oh good, a room of nightmares." Patty shut the door. She didn't see that one of the mannequin heads turned in her direction.

Abby walked down a narrow hallway. She saw flickering light under a door and slowly opened it. A familiar looking box was sitting in the middle of the room, sparking and humming. It reminded Abby of the device they'd found in the subway tunnel.

Abby spoke into her walkie. "Guys, I found another device."

Patty started to walk toward Abby. She didn't see that the mannequin followed her into the hallway.

"I had a good job," Patty muttered to herself. "Not a great job, but it was a good job." She heard something behind her. She stopped and turned. The mannequin stopped too. Patty looked at it curiously. "That wasn't there." She took a step toward it. Suddenly, the mannequin turned evil and charged at her!

"Oh, no way!" Patty yelled as she ran.

Meanwhile, Erin, Abby, and Holtzmann met in the storage room.

"It's definitely the same device we found in the subway," Abby said, looking closely.

"This is some sort of hyper-ionization device. Somebody's really trying to energize—" Erin started.

But at that moment, Patty ran in, slamming the door behind her and pressing her body in front of it. "I think I lost it. Please don't tell me that thing is unrelated to the ghost that we're looking for. I can't handle two things."

"What thing?" Erin asked.

A mannequin leg kicked through the door. Patty screamed. The Ghostbusters backed up and fired up their proton packs as the mannequin smashed through.

"I'm sorry, is this your dressing room?" Holtzmann asked the creature.

"Full para-transferral embodiment. Erin, all of our theories on spectral possession are true," Abby said.

Patty looked at them, then at the mannequin. "That's great, can we shoot it, now?"

Erin agreed. "There's a ghost inside that thing and I want it. Let's light him up!"

The Ghostbusters aimed their wands at the mannequin and fired. Their beams hit the mannequin, which glowed for a second, then exploded. A horrifying ghost screeched out and flew off down the hallway.

Erin had a determined look in her eyes when she rushed after it. "We can't lose it! C'mon."

"Wow, liking the fire," Abby said. Then she said to the others, "You heard her. Move it!"

The ghost flew down a hall. The Ghostbusters chased it. Erin fired her proton wand, but missed and blew a hole in the wall as the ghost disappeared through the ceiling.

"If we live through this, can you make these packs lighter, Holtz? My kidneys are taking a beating." Patty adjusted her pack.

Erin rushed up the stairs as Abby and Holtzmann hurried along to keep up.

Out in the theater, the crowd was booing Adam's band as they finished their first song. When they ended, the head of Thunder Gun Records shook his head.

Adam looked nervous. "We are the Beasts of Mayhem!" he announced to the audience, trying to get them excited. "And

 68

now let me ask you a question. Are you ready to rock?"

"You stink," a guy in the crowd called out.

And that was when the ghost rose out of the floor behind Adam and floated into the air!

"Wow," Eugene told Ely. "Adam really did spend some money. That's awesome."

The band started playing with more gusto. The audience was going crazy for the ghost.

The Ghostbusters hurried through a door and backstage. They looked out and saw that the ghost was circling above the crowd.

"Whoever made that device knows their high energy-density physics. That thing is *super* ionized," Erin said.

"And it is not benign," Abby added.

"It looks like it's looking for dinner." Patty did not want to be that meal.

Adam was at the front of the stage, pointing at the ghost, playing it up as if it was part of his show. "Behold the power of the Undead! For we are the Kings of Darkness!" The ghost took a dive straight for him.

Wham! The ghost sent him flying backward into a stack of amps. Adam whimpered, "Ow . . . I think I broke my tailbone."

Unsure if this was an act or not, the crowd cheered and the rest of the band kept playing.

69

Above the audience, the ghost continued circling like a vulture.

"Let's do this. Everybody ready?" Erin raised her wand.

"Yeah," Abby and Holtzmann said together.

"Um, sure," Patty said.

The Ghostbusters fired their beams, but they missed the ghost, hitting the elaborate ceiling instead. Plaster exploded and rained down on the audience, who applauded, loving every moment of this.

The ghost swiped Adam off the stage and carried him over the crowd.

"Help!" Adam shouted from high above the theater floor. "I think this thing is real! Help me!" He looked down to see the head of the record company watching, impressed. Adam regrouped. "I mean, help me keep. . . rocking you world! AAAAUGH!" The ghost dropped Adam.

The audience tried to catch the falling singer, but he hit them hard. A large group of rockers were knocked to the ground.

"It's gonna take a lot of fire power to pull that thing down," Holtzmann said.

"Circumvallate!" Erin suggested. "We need to surround it."

"Patty!" Abby barked orders. "Let's each take an aisle. Holtz, set the trap and let's reel that thing in."

 70

Abby and Patty rushed to the aisles as Erin and Holtzmann took up positions on the stage.

Patty shouted at everyone. "Get out of the way! We need to get down those aisles."

Abby took a microphone. "Guess what, people. You are now part of this operation. Patty, let's hit it." Like a rock star, Abby dove into the audience. They caught her and she body-surfed across the top of them.

"Left," Abby shouted. "Move me to the left. Now back. Keep going! Excellent!"

Patty was into it. "All right, you freaks. Time to catch a ghost. Let's do this!" Like Abby, she dove into the crowd, but everyone moved out of the way. She crashed onto the floor.

"How dare you let a lady hit the floor? Pick me up now!" Patty screeched. No one moved to help her. Patty didn't know that no one was getting close to her because there was a ghost standing on her shoulders.

"Just stay still," Abby told her.

"Patty, I—" Whatever Erin was going to say, Patty stopped her.

"No need to say anything."

"You—" Erin tried again.

"No," Patty protested. "I don't want to hear what you are about to say."

"But—" Holtzmann cut in.

"I'm pretty tired. I am actually just gonna take off," said Patty.

"I really don't think that's a good—" Erin said.

"Nope." Patty started up the aisle. "I'm out."

"Patty." Erin was firm. "Stay still!"

When Patty refused to stop, Abby said, "All right, ladies. Let's light it up. Fire. Just don't hit Patty!"

That made Patty stop. "What?" she cried.

As the other three Ghostbusters fired, the ghost jumped off Patty's shoulders. Patty realized what going on and drew her own wand. The ghost was struggling to escape the power of their beams. The band stopped playing. They had finally realized that this wasn't fake.

"Oh, I forgot to mention! Don't let your beam get entangled with my beam!" Holtzmann warned.

"What? Why?" Erin asked.

"It's too much power," Holtzmann explained. "It would cause a counter reaction. The beam will shoot back into your body and each atom will implode."

"WHAT?" Erin freaked out.

 72

Holtzmann ignored her. "Okay, I'm gonna open the trap on three, everyone else hold steady." She flipped open the trap with her foot, then kicked it toward the foot of the stage. The inside of the trap lit up into a wide glowing tractor beam.

"Okay! Bring it down!" Holtzmann said.

They slowly lowered the ghost ensnared in their streams.

"Turn off your streams as soon as I close the trap. Ready? Okay . . . off!" Holtzmann stomped her foot on the trigger, the ghost was sucked inside, and the lid slammed shut. Steam rose from the trap.

The Ghostbusters all lowered their beams while Holtzmann lifted the box by the cord. They stared at her.

"Are you waiting for me to say something?" she asked them.

"Did we catch a ghost or not?" Erin asked.

"Oh, we caught a ghost." Holtzmann grinned.

The Ghostbusters jumped around the stage shouting, "Yes!" and "We did it!"

Erin and Abby hugged. The crowd went wild and the band started playing again.

Holtzmann picked up a guitar and smashed it. She apologized to the guitar player, "Sorry, got caught up in the moment."

Erin kissed the ghost trap.

73

"Erin, that's radioactive," Abby warned.

Erin looked worried.

Holtzmann said, "It's okay, you'll just take some potassium iodine for the next ten years. It's fine." She gave a look to Abby, like in the subway tunnel and mouthed, "It's not good."

From backstage, the famous rock star Ozzy Osborne watched the action. He packed up his gear to leave, saying, "I can't follow that."

The Ghostbusters were heroes. As they left the theater, a massive crowd cheered for them. The NY News vans were there to capture the moment. Erin couldn't stop smiling. It was the best day of her life.

CHAPTER 10

It was time to celebrate. At the Ghostbusters' headquarters, the stereo was blaring and Erin and Patty danced.

Erin danced over to Kevin. "C'mon, Kevin! Let's see what you've got."

"Give us something!" Patty circled around him.

Kevin joined in the fun and the three of them danced over to where Abby and Holtzmann were at a workbench, taking apart the strange sparking device they'd found in the theater.

Erin tried to get them to dance. "Guys. It's time to celebrate. This is what 'legit' feels like." She grabbed the trap and gave it another kiss.

"Okay, you gotta stop kissing the trap," Abby warned.

"I know. But it's like, the more you guys say 'Don't kiss the trap,' the more I want to kiss the trap." Erin raised the trap to Holtzmann. "Get in on this!"

Holtzmann had moved to her workbench. "Rain check. Exciting things happening over here. Newly printed circuit boards, superconducting magnets rebuilt, beam accuracy improved and extended by producing a controlled plasma inside a new RF discharge chamber in the redesigned wand, a cryocooler to reduce helium boil-off. And—wait for it—a Faraday cage to attenuate RF noise and provide physical protection to avoid quenches. Can I get a 'woot woot'?"

"Woot woot!" Abby and Erin cheered.

Kevin interrupted the celebration. "Ummmm. There's someone here to see you. Some debunker or something."

"Someone?" Erin thought about it for a second, then said, "You mean Martin Heiss? The famed scientist? The paranormal debunker? Here? Inside this building?"

The Ghostbusters followed Kevin to where Heiss was standing, looking at all the maps and notes filled with scientific notations, equations, and crazy squiggles tacked on the wall.

"Mr. Heiss, welcome to our laboratory," Erin greeted.

Heiss turned toward them. "Is now a bad time?"

"Actually, it is—" Abby started.

"Not at all. Please, have a seat." Erin cut in. She called across the office space, "Kevin, could you please get Mr. Heiss some water?"

Heiss sat down in a chair. The Ghostbusters joined him.

"I sure hope you don't mind being recorded," he said, holding a camera.

Erin was uncomfortable. "Well, I actually would prefer—" He hit record and she gave in. "Oh, okay."

Kevin handed Heiss a glass of water that was only one-eighth full. It was an odd choice. Heiss took a long look at the glass, then turned his attention to the Ghostbusters. "Let's start light and easy. Ever hear of the One Million Dollar Paranormal Challenge? James Randi offered to pay one million dollars to anyone who can prove paranormal claims under scientific testing criteria. No one has. Why are you pretending to catch ghosts?"

Abby was outraged. "We only know what *four percent* of the universe—"

"Breathe," Erin told Abby. Then to Heiss she said, "Sir, we believe in the scientific method. I've dedicated my life to it. We have been working on bringing the paranormal into a controlled environment so we can supply that proof. This has been very difficult to do. But we have now done just that." She gestured to the ghost trap. "At four thirty-two p.m. today we successfully trapped a class three vapor."

"You're saying there's a ghost in that box?" Heiss asked pointedly.

"Yes, I am," Erin told him.

"Well, I would just love to see it. Wouldn't that be a treat?" His tone was mocking.

"You can't," Abby said. "We still have to establish the best method of testing that can contain it in the lab."

"What a shame." Heiss wrote something on a notepad.

"Otherwise, we would show you," Erin assured him.

Heiss said, "Hey. You gotta keep it contained. What can you do?"

"Listen, I know this sounds like we're making it up." Erin gestured at their jumpsuits and packs in a corner. "Obviously, we look a little ridiculous right now."

"You look like the Orkin of fake," Heiss said, referencing the famous exterminator company.

Patty stood. "Well, it was real nice of you to stop by."

Erin was angry. "You wanna see it?" she asked. Maybe it was time to let the ghost out of the bag—or trap, as it were.

"I would love to see it," Heiss told her.

 78

"Too bad. He can't," Abby told Erin.

"I think he should see it," Erin insisted.

"This jerk's approval doesn't matter. There are more import-ant things at play," Abby whispered to her.

"I bet," Heiss said under his breath.

Erin reached out to the trap. "We're showing him."

Holtzmann and Patty put on their proton packs, ready to recapture the ghost.

Erin told Heiss, "I would stand over here behind us."

"I weirdly think I'll be just fine here." He stayed put.

Abby blocked Erin's hand. "Erin, no. We finally caught this entity. I'm not letting you do this."

"Okay. Fine, fine. I get it," Erin said as Abby said, "Good."

Then in a flash, Erin hit the button on the trap. Everyone gasped.

Nothing happened. No ghost.

"Oh, come on." Erin tapped the box with her foot. Still nothing. She was confused.

Martin turned off his camera. "Well, it was lovely meet-ing y—"

Suddenly, the ghost flew out of the box. It lifted Martin Heiss in the air and threw him out the window. The ghost then left through the opening, zooming off into the night.

79

The Ghostbusters ran to the window.

"Oh no!" Patty gasped. This was not good.

It didn't take long for the police to arrive. An ambulance took Martin Heiss away.

"I'm going to ask you one more time," Officer Stevenson interrogated the Ghostbusters. "And if you tell me a ghost threw him out the window again, you will be answering this behind bars. So, here we go. What happened?"

"Ghost did it," Holtzmann mumbled.

"Say that louder please?" the officer said. "I just want to be sure I'm hearing you right."

Just as he was ready to arrest them, several black SUVs pulled up. Two men in suits flashed badges to the cops.

Agent Frank Hawkins spoke first. "Official business. We've got this."

"You need to come with us," Agent Rorke told the Ghostbusters.

"Why? Who are you guys?" Erin asked.

"The mayor would like a word," Hawkins replied.

Thirty minutes later, the Ghostbusters were standing in the mayor's office. Mayor Bradley was sitting at his desk.

His spokeswoman, Jennifer Lynch, stood nearby.

The mayor welcomed them. "There they are. Sorry for all this drama. Please, have a seat."

"Listen, something big is happening. We're not frauds. We are scientists," Erin assured him.

"We know you're not frauds, because we've been monitoring the situation as well," the mayor said.

Ms. Lynch explained, "Agents Hawkins and Rorke are with Homeland Security. We've been investigating this extremely quietly."

"So, what do you know?" the mayor asked them.

"Um, just that we believe someone is creating devices to attract and amplify paranormal activity," Erin told him.

"And this activity could be escalating toward a larger-scale event," Abby added.

"Well, that sounds terrible. I certainly don't like the sound of that," the mayor said. "Okay. Well, listen. Thank you. Great work. Really. But it's time to knock it off."

"Excuse me?" Abby rubbed her ears.

"These gentlemen are on it." The mayor nodded toward the agents. "Let the government do its work."

"The mayor's concern is that you're drawing too much attention to yourselves," Ms. Lynch said.

"I think we keep a pretty low profile," Erin assured him.

Agent Hawkins narrowed his eyes. "You drive a hearse with a ghost on it. You use an unauthorized siren. Do you know how many federal regulations you are breaking on a daily basis?"

"We're going to have to make the public believe you're frauds," the mayor told them.

"What?" Erin's face was flushed. That was the last thing she wanted to hear.

"The human mind can only handle so much," Ms. Lynch began. "If people knew what was happening right now, there would be a panic. We'll have to put out information that the concert incident was a hoax. Otherwise, there would be mass hysteria."

Abby said, "Listen, all we care about is being able to continue to do our work."

"Now, that's true," Erin said. "But it just seems like all those people already saw what happened and what we did. It must be all over the internet by now."

"You mean a bunch of metal heads who saw a high-tech prop that went out of control? And then their cell phone photos were all erased by a magnetic wave blast? We've got it covered," Agent Rorke said.

"Wow." Abby couldn't believe they had such an elaborate plan.

"It's just . . . if we could just back up one second . . . can't there be both things? And I'm just spit-balling here—but like, what if we told people what we did, but then said it's all under control?" Erin was trying to solve the problem.

Abby shook her head. "I think Ms. Lynch here made it very clear we don't want mass hysteria."

"Okay, okay. Fair enough," Erin said. "But what is 'mass hysteria'? I mean, is it really that bad?"

"Let me show you a clip of it." Jennifer Lynch hit play on a video on her laptop.

The images of screaming mobs that appeared on her screen were horrible.

"Why would you even have that on your laptop?" Patty asked, covering her eyes.

"Right, right," Erin said as the video ended. "It's just, I feel like the cat's already sort of out of the bag."

"Are you finished?" Abby asked.

"The cat's been out of the bag before and yet people always get bored and put it back in." Agent Rorke gave examples. "A police officer in New Mexico reports a UFO encounter. The crew of the *SS Ourang Medan* mysteriously dies. The entire town of Langville, Montana goes missing."

"What? I never heard of that," Erin said.

The mayor ended the meeting, addressing the Ghostbusters. "Well, on that horrifying note, thank you all so much for what you've done. We will always be grateful for your service. Please think of me as a friend." He quickly added, "A friend who will ignore you on the street, but a friend nonetheless."

"A long distance friend." Jennifer Lynch opened the door for them.

"Exactly. A pen pal. But without letters. Or any kind of contact. Never send me anything in writing," the mayor said.

Ms. Lynch led them out. "Hawkins and Rorke will escort you home. We'll speak to you soon."

CHAPTER 11

Later the Ghostbusters watched Jennifer Lynch being interviewed on TV.

"It's fraudulent and unsafe. These 'Ghostbusters' are just creating an unnecessary panic in a sad grab for fame. We went to their lab—there's absolutely nothing there. People can rest assured that these women are just bored and sad."

Abby, Holtzmann, and Patty were somehow able to control their emotions, while Erin fumed. Frustrated, she shoved the equipment worktable. It crashed to the ground.

Kevin asked, "Guys, what was that thing before?"

"It was a ghost," Holtzmann said. "What do you think goes on here?"

"I didn't know. I answer the phone in a Chinese restaurant where four women sit around in painters' outfits. When people ask me what I do, my response is, 'I have no idea.' I guess I knew it had something to do with Chinese food and science. I couldn't put it together." Kevin scratched his head.

"This is a very serious news report. . . ." Patty pointed at the TV.

"Painting us as delusional frauds," Erin said sadly.

"So what? We're not." Abby was still confident that they could make it all work.

Erin was filled with doubt. "But nobody knows that! In fact, look, it says 'frauds' right there on the screen." The words were right under their picture.

"But that doesn't make it true," Abby said. She gave Erin a pep talk.

"Last week we saw a class four malevolent apparition. And then we came back here, and we figured out how to catch one. And it worked. Who cares what anyone else says? We know what we're doing. There are bigger issues at play here." She went to the computer. "Look!"

Abby read the report aloud. "A wailing spirit sighted on sixth and twenty-sixth. A spectral polar bear on Park and forty-fifth. Weeping walls at a thrift store in Chelsea. Someone's clearly trying to break open the barrier and unleash the dead, and we need to—"

Erin suddenly raised her head, interested in what Abby was saying. "Wait. Sixth and twenty-sixth?"

She looked around the room, then jumped up and ripped down the New York map that had been tacked to the wall. "Where'd we find the first device?"

"At the subway," Patty said.

Erin bent over the map. "Here's the theater. Give me the other sightings." Abby read the addresses and she filled in the map, drawing two lines straight through Manhattan.

"What do those look like to you?" Erin asked the others.

"I can't see," Kevin said, still rubbing his eyes.

"Ley lines," Abby and Holtzmann said at the same time.

"What are ley lines?" Patty asked.

"A hidden network of energy lines across the Earth. Currents of supernatural energy. Let me see if there's a ley line map of New York City," Abby said.

"Supposedly if you look at sacred sites and weird events around the world, you can draw a line between them. And where lines intersect create an unusually powerful spot. Abby and I always dismissed it, because it seemed too likely to happen at random to have any merit."

Holtzmann pulled an old ley line map book from under a pile. Abby overlaid it with her marked New York City map. The lines matched up perfectly.

"I guess there is some merit," Abby said. They were on the edge of a dangerous discovery.

"He's been using those devices to charge up the ley lines," Erin said about whoever was behind this recent increase in hauntings. "He's creating a vortex!"

"If he has something powerful enough in here, he could rip a hole right through the barrier," Abby declared.

"Letting everything out there, come in here!" Holtzmann paced the room.

"What's there now?" Patty asked, looking at the site where the ley lines intersected on the map.

"The Mercado," Holtzmann said.

"The Mercado." Patty considered it. "Well, that makes sense."

"Why's that?" Holtzmann asked.

Patty went on to explain. "The Mercado has one of the weirdest histories of any building in New York City. Check out these online reviews." She scrolled to the page and turned the computer. "'Half a star: I felt strange there.' 'Loud noises in my closet throughout the night.'"

 88

Holtzmann asked Patty, "So it's a haunted building?"

"Nah, this is even before it was a building. All sorts of massacres happened there," Patty said. "Like a peaceful trade with Captain Warren and the Lenape Indians, and suddenly everyone dies." She went on, "You know, no other section of New York has more power outages? Also a ton of pedestrian deaths. My cousin got hit by a car in front of there. But he's an idiot."

Erin stood at the computer with Patty. They were looking at the Mercado's website. There was a picture of the entire staff standing in the lobby smiling. Only one person was straight-faced. . . . It was Rowan in his maintenance uniform.

"Hold on!" Patty poked a finger at the screen. "That's the dude from the subway! Talking about cataclysms."

"Bingo," Erin shouted.

"Fire up the car and let's get over to this hotel of horrors." Abby started gathering equipment.

The Ecto-1 screeched to a stop in front of the Mercado. The Ghostbusters jumped out and headed in. At the front desk, the clerk was on the phone.

"And did you try adjusting the thermostat before making

this call? Oh, what a wonderful tone you've decided to use with me. I see the cold draft has not cooled your temperament."

"Excuse me," Erin interrupted.

The desk clerk turned toward them and raised a finger, silently asking for a minute. Then into the phone, he said, "Uh-huh. Well that sounds more like a *you* problem. Hold on." To the Ghostbusters, he asked, "What do you want?"

"Where's your janitor?" Abby asked.

"Ugh, that guy? What has he done?" The clerk pointed to where they could find Rowan. "I don't care. Take the stairs down."

The Ghostbusters rushed to the door, down the stairs, and to the metal door of the boiler room. Beneath the door, a light flashed. They readied their proton packs and entered.

The first thing they all saw was the mirror. Behind the glass, glimpses of nightmarish ghosts were trying to break free. The creepy sounds were terrifying.

Rowan was there too. His fingers flew over a keyboard connected to a large machine that seemed to be controlling the ghosts.

"Stop!" Abby stepped forward. "Okay, I know you're having a ball bringing all these ghosts into New York, but the thing is, we happen to like this world the way it is."

"I don't," Rowan replied. "I think it's garbage. And when the barrier is destroyed, the armies of the undead will return to pester the living."

"'Pester' doesn't sound too bad—" Erin said.

"They will pester the living with unspeakable pain and torment. Everyone will be eliminated," Rowan went on.

"Different meaning of 'pester,'" Erin acknowledged.

"Yeah. That's something else," Holtzmann agreed.

Abby went for the compassionate approach. "You don't like people? People can do terrible things. I get it. Don't get me started on this one." She gave a small nod toward Erin. "But then there's good things! All sorts of good things like, like soup and . . . hmm, why is the only thing I can think about soup?! I'm very stressed out. Just stop the machine!"

Rowan brushed her off and turned up the power.

Abby pointed her proton wand at him. Rowan froze.

They all heard sirens wailing outside the hotel.

"Don't take another step!" Abby warned Rowan. "The police are on their way down."

"Well, in that case . . . bye." Rowan grabbed onto the electrified ghostly mist his machine was creating and electrocuted himself. He fell to the floor—dead.

91

The Ghostbusters were stunned.

"What?" Erin didn't know what else to say.

"Turn the machine off!" Abby told Holtzmann. She ran over to shut it down. They all looked at Rowan's body.

Holtzmann frowned. "Weird move."

"Holtz, are we okay?" Erin asked.

Holtzmann read the machine meters. "Yeah, I think so."

"Well, at least it's over." Erin continued to look at Rowan.

Abby called up to the police, "Hey! Down here!"

Police and Homeland Security surrounded the Mercado. Erin walked over to Abby, who was now looking at Rowan's ghost machine.

"What's up?" Erin asked.

"It's so strange, a lot of his technology isn't that different from ours. It's the same science behind our apparition catching," Abby said.

"That is strange." Erin looked closer.

"I think I know why that is." Holtzmann was holding a book from Rowan's bedside table. It was the one Abby and Erin had written.

"Well, it's a very powerful book," Abby said.

Jennifer Lynch entered the room. "Thank you for everything you've done. You saved us all. The mayor privately thanks you as well. Let me walk you out."

As they walked out, Erin watched the police and Homeland Security forces dismantling Rowan's machine. She breathed a sigh of relief. The vortex would be closed. The danger was over . . . or was it?

CHAPTER 12

Hawkins and Rorke were waiting by the door to the Mercado.

"Now, you get some rest," Ms. Lynch told the Ghostbusters. "Let these guys get you out of here."

"That sounds nice, thank you," Abby said.

"I just have to say a few words. You know how it is." Jennifer Lynch opened the door, revealing the press waiting outside. Agents Rorke and Hawkins moved to arrest the Ghostbusters, while Jennifer told the reporters, "Everything's fine, just another publicity stunt by these incredibly sad, lonely women. I mean, give it a rest, am I right?"

//////////////////////

Back in the Mercado basement, Homeland Security agents finished putting up crime scene tape around the disassembled machine and sealed the maintenance room. In the chaos, Abby had left her PKE meter on the floor. The indicators slowly began to blink.

The Ghostbusters were let go near Times Square. Since it was over, they wanted to celebrate.

"Mission accomplished. Let's celebrate." Abby grinned wildly while Holtzmann and Patty high-fived. Erin looked bummed and preoccupied.

"Erin, you in?" Abby asked her. "My treat."

A blogger from the press conference caught up to them. He was holding up his phone to record the impromptu interview. "How do you feel about wasting tax payer money and government resources with your pranks?"

Abby got between him and Erin. "Back off, buddy. We've got nothing to say to the press."

He got closer to Erin. "Miss Gilbert, I asked around your hometown. Talked to someone you went to school with. They told me when you were a kid you made up a ghost. Tell me, were you born a fraud, 'ghost girl?'"

Erin lost her cool. She lunged at the reporter.

95

Abby grabbed her, pulling her back. "Whoa, whoa! Let it go!"

But Erin was out of control. She snagged the blogger's shirt, while Patty and Holtzmann tried to stop her.

"You freak!" the blogger shouted as he broke free. Erin chased him down the street, and when she caught up, she punched him in the nose.

The next morning's newspaper had a huge photo of Erin punching the blogger. The headline read: NOSEBUSTERS! She pushed back the paper and buried her face in her hands.

Holtzmann came in, taking off her proton gloves. "I'm working on some new treats. No spoilers. But let's just say I've always wanted to throw a proton grenade." She casually reached over for the newspaper and started reading.

Erin waited for her reaction, but Holtzmann didn't say a word. She just sipped her coffee and flipped pages. She finally said, "These guys really have their finger on the pulse."

"Just read it to me," Erin sighed.

"Okay." Holtzmann read the article out loud. "'Midtown movie theater owner claims basset hound regularly attends matinees by himself.'"

Erin groaned. "The story about me."

"Oh." Holtzmann flipped back to the front page. "I really didn't notice. . . ." She read a bit to herself. "It's not that interesting."

Erin turned on the TV's local newscast.

The reporter was saying, "We spoke to Harold Filmore, Physics Department Chair at Columbia University, where Ms. Gilbert used to teach. . . ."

"Oh no," Erin sighed heavily.

The camera switched over to Dr. Filmore's office at the university. Behind Dr. Filmore, the blogger's video was playing. Erin looked like a maniac.

"It's unfortunate that we have these former ties with Ms. Gilbert," Filmore said. "At Columbia University, we're about real science, discovering truths, not lying for a sad moment of fame."

The blogger's cell phone video froze on a particularly insane and unattractive frame of Erin.

Abby came in. "Doesn't matter what those people think."

Then the news anchor said, "We also spoke with the Dean of the Kenneth P. Higgins Institute."

The camera moved to an image of the dean at his desk, finishing his sack lunch.

"A terrible shame on the Kenneth P. Higgins name."

Patty turned off the TV. "Forget those dudes. You gotta just walk that off. Think about how many people you saved."

"Yeah, let's just grab something to eat and find that basset hound," Holtzmann suggested.

Erin had to get away. "I think I'm gonna take a walk." She left alone.

Kevin approached Abby at her desk, saying, "Hey, Abby, can we talk about the paranormal? I got a bunch of ideas and theories about—"

"Not now, Kevin." Abby left the room.

Kevin walked back to his desk with a frown.

At Columbia University, Dr. Filmore was in his office, at his desk. Erin was showing him her files and explaining about the proton pack. He seemed interested. . . .

"Of course in a million years if someone asked if I believed in ley lines, I would've said no. But as you can see, the incidents lined up. Our equipment is real. We really saved New York City."

"Oh, Erin," Filmore said with enthusiasm. "I had no idea. This evidence is undeniable. I have to apologize for doubting you. Would you ever consider rejoining us? You can head up a legitimate science-based paranormal department."

Erin beamed. "Yes. Yes, I would. Thank you, sir." She was back where she wanted to be.

"Thank *you*," Filmore said, and then he glanced behind her.

 98

Erin's heart sank as two security guards entered and grabbed her arms.

"What took you so long?" Filmore asked them as the guards led Erin out of his office. "That was uncomfortable."

If Erin thought being fired was bad, being escorted out by security was worse. She struggled to carry her proton pack and files.

Playing it off, she called back to Filmore, "Okay, so we'll just finish that up later."

People in the hallway avoided eye contact.

"Look, I'm not crazy," Erin told anyone who would listen. "I know when people say that, they're usually crazy, but I'm pointing that out, so I obviously have an intelligent perspective in the situation."

Security left Erin on the street. She didn't know where to go next or what to do, when Abby arrived.

"So, how'd that go?" Abby asked.

Erin let out a long breath.

"You just can't handle those scientists thinking we're a big joke," Abby said.

Erin slumped onto a bench, putting the proton pack by her feet. "Is that some sort of big reveal? Yes, that bothers me. I don't like being dragged through the mud. I mean, any shot of being on a faculty or having any kind of reputation is gone. Believe it or not, my dream was not to start a ghost detective agency above a Chinese restaurant. I mean, Abby, we don't even look like idiots, we look like maniacs. I know you don't care, but I do!"

Abby, usually so calm, exploded with frustration and anger. "You think I don't care? You think it's been easy, devoting my life to all this? Of course I care. I've been called 'weird' every day of my life since I was four years old, and I hate it. But I focus on what matters. We discovered all sorts of new things. I get to work with my friends. I felt pretty lucky. The only thing that makes me sad is that after all this time, you haven't changed one bit!"

"Well, I'm not going to take that as an insult, because I happen to like myself," Erin said, rising.

"No, you don't," Abby said.

Erin slunk back down onto the bench. That hurt.

"Take care of yourself," Abby said, then she walked away.

As she passed a few students, they snickered at her Ghostbusters uniform, but Abby kept her head up high and kept on walking.

CHAPTER 13

Erin was getting ready for bed. She tossed her Ghostbusters uniform into the laundry basket, then sat down at the computer and went online. She clicked on the old University of Michigan interview, the one Abby did alone after she didn't show up.

The host asked Abby snarky questions about their book, while Abby looked uncomfortable.

"So, you're saying that ghosts are actually real? And you can back this up with science? What could be less scientific than that? Have you actually ever even seen a ghost?" he asked, face filled with doubt.

"We have . . . um. . . I mean . . ." Abby was nervous and

sputtering. "I have experienced . . . um . . . theoretical contact with . . . the . . . um . . . spirit world."

"I'm sorry but I find that hard to—" the host was saying when Erin turned the video off. She picked up a copy of her and Abby's book and looked at their photo.

Flipping through a few pages, Erin realized that this was not her copy of the book. It was Rowan's. His notes were scribbled inside.

She shuddered, thinking about how she'd last seen him. Turning pages, Erin noticed that in a chapter called "Attracting the Paranormal," Rowan had sketched a design for his massive machine on the page. "The First Cataclysm" was written underneath.

A few more pages in, Erin found an illustration of an electrocution. Another few pages and Rowan had circled the words: "Vengeful Spirits and the Dangers of their Return to Our World." By the time Erin reached the last pages, she discovered an intricate vision of ghosts terrorizing New York City. There was one massive being in the background.

The drawing was of Rowan himself, with the headline: "The Fourth Cataclysm—I will lead them."

"Oh no," Erin muttered.

Abby sat in an almost empty lab, staring sadly at a picture of her and Erin onstage at the rock concert, holding the smoking ghost trap.

Holtzmann and Patty put on their coats.

"Holtz and I are gonna pick up a snack, something light," Patty told Abby. "Probably a cheesesteak. Want one?"

Abby frowned. "I'm good, thanks." After they left, Abby's eyes drifted to the empty spot where Erin's proton pack should have been. She looked quickly away, then headed to the bathroom.

A knock on the front door made her stop.

"Did you forget your keys again? Wear them on a lanyard." Abby opened the door. There was no one there. She checked the hall. Empty. "Very funny," she said, as if it were one of Holtzmann's pranks. "Spooky."

She closed the door and started to the bathroom again.

Another knock.

"What are we? In kindergarten?" She opened the door again, saying, "I'm not in the mood."

No one was there. The hall was dark. She shut the door one more time, and this time, bolted it shut. Then she hurried to the bathroom.

When the knock came for the third time, it was on the

bathroom door. She turned the lock and stumbled back against the sink.

"Who is that?!"

She had her eyes on the door when a rattling noise came from the sink. She leaned in slowly to look at the drain.

Something flew out of the pipes and into Abby's face. She screamed and fell backward, ectoplasm dripping out of her nose and ears. She grabbed her stomach and vomited ecto-plasm across the room.

Abby fell to the floor, just as the answering machine began to play her outgoing message. "Hello. You have reached the Ghostbusters hotline. Please leave your name, number, a description of your apparition, a description of what you were doing at the time of encountering the apparition, and a description of the actual encounter with said apparition—"

BEEP.

Erin was pacing in her apartment. She yelled into her phone, "Abby? Come on! Shorten that greeting. It's Erin. Call me back. I think killing himself was just the next step in his plan!"

She looked at her TV. It said, "'Dinner with the Mayor" over the anchor's head. Erin turned up the volume. The anchor

said, "Mayor Bradley is meeting with the diplomats at Lotus Leaf on—"

She hung up the phone and dashed to the door.

Holtzmann and Patty returned to headquarters, carrying the takeout.

Patty called out to Abby, "We got you a cheesesteak, because we don't want you picking off of ours. Come and get it."

"Hey, Abby. You in there?" Holtzmann knocked on the bathroom door. "Abby? Everything all right?"

Abby came out. "Hey," she said, a bit too casually.

"You okay?" Holtzmann squinted at her.

"I'm quite well," Abby said.

"Well, good." Holtzmann said, then she looked to Patty and shrugged. "Not our best back and forth." She then noticed that Abby was standing by the proton packs, looking at them curiously.

Abby picked up a metal pipe that Holtzmann had found in a Dumpster. With speed and strength, she started beating the packs with the pipe. Parts were flying everywhere!

"What are you doing?" Holtzmann hurried over and grabbed Abby's arms, making her drop the pipe.

Abby swept Holtzmann up by the throat and carried her

105

to the window, crashing through the glass, and dangling her feet over the sidewalk below.

"You guys aren't playing a game, are you?" Patty knocked Abby against the wall and grabbed Holtzmann's hand. Abby attacked her as Patty struggled to pull Holtzmann back into the room.

Abby and Patty slammed each other back and forth as Patty tried to hold onto Holtzmann and fight off Abby at the same time. Finally, Patty managed to sweep Abby's leg, knocking her down. Having gained the upper hand, Patty yanked Holtzmann back inside, then pinned Abby down, twisting her arm behind her and shouting, "Get out of my friend, evil spirit!"

Patty smacked Abby across the face as hard as she could.

The ghost of Rowan exploded out of Abby's body. The windows shattered with an otherworldly sonic boom as he flew outside.

Abby looked around the room, which appeared to have been through a mighty battle, then felt her face. "OUCH!"

Patty smacked Abby across the face again.

"STOP! It's me. What part of 'ouch' didn't you understand?" Abby asked.

Patty backed off.

Kevin's voice boomed from outside on the street. "Hey, guys! Check it out!"

Holtzmann and Patty went to the hole where the window once was and looked out as Abby struggled to her feet. Kevin was sitting on a junky motorcycle that was painted white with a Ghostbusters logo on the side. He was wearing a homemade jumpsuit, looking like one of them.

"I figure you're going to need my help. I just need my own proton pack, if you could—"

Abby got to the window just in time to see Rowan's ghost circling Kevin. "Kevin! Get inside!"

"I really don't appreciate being yelled at like that—" He didn't finish before Rowan's ghost entered his body. Kevin looked down at his body as if seeing it for the first time.

"Thanks for the upgrade," Kevin/Rowan said. "This will be very helpful." With that, he revved up the motorcycle and peeled out, racing down the street.

"Oh, that's not good," Patty said as he rounded a corner and disappeared.

CHAPTER 14

Mayor Bradley was dining with Jennifer Lynch and several dignitaries at the Lotus Leaf restaurant. Jennifer spotted Erin running down the sidewalk.

"Oh boy, code red," she told the mayor quietly.

"What is this woman doing?" the mayor asked.

"Maybe she just really likes this restaurant?" Jennifer suggested.

As soon as Erin was inside, she dashed over to Mayor Bradley and Jennifer. "You have to evacuate the city!"

"Don't say that word. *Never* say that word," the mayor whispered sharply. Then he acted as if he'd never seen Erin before. "Ma'am, I don't believe we've met."

Erin blurted, "It's not over. It's just beginning. I don't know how he's going to do it, but you gotta send every officer over to the Mercado and you have to shut down the power to the city."

"I'm sorry, as you can see, the mayor is at dinner right now." Jennifer shooed her away.

A large rumbling outside made everyone turn.

"It's already starting," Erin said. But when they looked, it was just a garbage Dumpster being wheeled by. "Oh. Okay, but it's still starting, though."

Two guards snagged Erin and began to drag her off.

"That took way too long," the mayor said.

"No!" Erin shrieked, hanging onto Mayor Bradley's table as the guards tried to pull her away. She wouldn't budge.

"This is crazy," Jennifer told Erin. "You're embarrassing yourself."

"I . . . don't . . . care!" Erin was hanging onto the table as the guards held up her feet. She was clutching the table so hard, it started dragging through the restaurant with her.

Finally, Erin let go and they chased her to the door, where she escaped, leaving the mayor and his guests stunned.

"Never a dull moment!" Mayor Bradley said with a forced laugh.

Kevin, possessed with Rowan's ghost, approached the generator room at the Mercado Hotel. Two cops were on guard duty at the door.

109

One officer stopped him. "Hey, you can't come back here."

"Interesting. Is that so?" Kevin/Rowan punched one cop, then the other. They both dropped, unconscious.

"I should have worked out more when I was alive," Kevin/Rowan said, flexing Kevin's muscles.

He kicked open the door and entered the room.

Kevin/Rowan found the larger pieces of his machine and inspected them. He was pleased with Kevin's strong body as he lifted the heavy parts easily.

"I *definitely* should have worked out more," he said. Kevin's body was just right for his plan.

He fit the pieces into the machine, then hit a switch. It fired up, filling the room with sparks and lightning.

Ka-boom!

The mirrors all exploded as paranormal lights and spirits rocketed into the world.

Erin was headed to the Mercado when suddenly the ground trembled. The people she passed looked worried. A loud boom echoed through the sky.

At headquarters, Holtzmann was hurriedly fixing the proton packs that Abby had broken while possessed.

"Are they ready?" Abby asked every few seconds. "We've got

 110

to get to the Mercado and save Kevin. As if he hasn't been through enough already."

Holtzmann was working as fast as she could. "If you weren't so strong, you would have done much less damage to these."

"I'm sorry I got possessed!" Abby said. "I guess I should have thought that through more." She picked up the phone and dialed. "Erin! Where are you? Rowan took Kevin. We need your help!" She hung up and groaned. "What a surprise. Never there when you need her."

Erin was running toward Times Square, but people and cars were all fleeing in the opposite direction. The Mercado was still a ways in the distance. Above the building, red clouds gathered in the sky, turning the day into night. Ghosts poured out of the building, dispersing throughout Manhattan.

"I need my gear," Erin said to herself. She ran to the curb and waved down a taxi.

"Where you going?" the driver asked.

"Chinatown."

"Nah."

Meanwhile, all around New York, ghosts were creating chaos.

A couple ran around a corner, screaming as a skeleton chased them.

A woman hurried into a subway station and found a stream of ghost rats.

In a coffee shop, patrons rushed to the window to see what was going on.

Professor Filmore was in that coffee shop. He looked over at the guy next to him. At first he didn't register what he saw, but after a few moments, he realized it wasn't a guy next to him. It was a *ghost*. Filmore screamed and ran out into the street.

Police, SWAT, and the National Guard gathered at the Mercado, weapons drawn. Large glowing cracks were forming in the sidewalk from underneath the building. Agents Hawkins and Rorke moved in with confidence.

"Don't worry! Everything is going to be okay!" Hawkins told the crowd, then into a headset, he said, "Bring it out."

A big military truck rumbled through the street with a giant proton cannon attached.

Two police officers approached Hawkins.

"What is that thing? Do you guys know what you're doing?" one asked.

 112

"You've tested this thing, right?" The other wanted to know.

Rorke pushed them away. "Stand back, friend. We've got a city to save."

Agent Hawkins fired the cannon. The beam hit the building. The cracks from underneath the building grew. The building shone brighter. The cannon was making things worse.

Kevin/Rowan floated down onto a ledge and raised his arms. He was glowing.

"Dear brave men of the protection services industry, thank you for coming to my party, but instead of fighting . . . I would like to see you dance." With that, the Bee Gees' song, "You Should Be Dancing," began to play.

Shining blurs of light shot out of Kevin/Rowan's hands down at the troops. Hawkins and Rorke were standing in front and were hit with the first rays of the blast.

The cops and soldiers all jolted as the blurs absorbed into their chests.

Kevin/Rowan stood in a disco pose.

They all took the same pose.

When Kevin/Rowan started disco dancing, everyone joined in—all under his control.

Hawkins and Rorke were powerless as they boogied to the beat.

113

CHAPTER 15

The Ecto-1 peeled out of Ghostbusters' headquarters at top speed. In the distance, the Mercado building was glowing. Massive supernatural clouds roiled above it.

Ecto-1 drove along, dodging people fleeing down the street.

Patty grabbed the intercom. "Respect the siren, please."

The crowd didn't care. They swarmed past Ecto-1, blocking their way.

"Hey! We're trying to save you, so get out of the way!" Patty told them.

The crowd started to thin, but now pretzel and hot dog carts blocked the way. The three Ghostbusters leaped out of the Ecto-1 to help move them aside, only to discover Slimer, a squat green ghost, was inside one of the carts eating hot dogs.

"Whoa!" Abby said as the ghost jumped into the Ecto-1 and stole their car. He wasn't a good driver, hitting anything and anyone in the way.

"Well . . . I guess we're walking," Abby said with a shrug.

Patty, Holtzmann, and Abby power-walked up a New York street, passing people running in the other direction.

In the distance they saw a huge crowd of ghosts watching a parade, but it wasn't a modern parade—it was an eerie parade from the 1920s. Balloons that looked like weird cats, strange insects, and a disturbing Pinocchio floated above the parade route. An odd Santa and a creepy elf balloon came into view.

"People had a much higher tolerance for creepy back then," Patty noted.

"Still, at least a parade is something happy. Keep them busy and in a good mood," Abby said, but she spoke too soon. A beat later, the balloons turned toward the Ghostbusters and started chasing them.

"Pop some balloons! Now!" Abby shouted.

The Ghostbusters started firing, exploding some and popping holes in others so they flew away. A giant Stay-Puft Marshmallow Man balloon was hit. He crashed down on them, smothering the Ghostbusters under his belly.

"I can't reach the trigger," Abby huffed.

"This isn't exactly how I pictured my death," Holtzmann gasped.

"Smothered by a class six possession with temporal displacement?" Abby asked her.

"Oh, it's class six? No, never mind," Holtzmann said.

Suddenly, the Stay-Puft Man burst into a shower of shredded balloon.

When the dust settled, it was clear that Erin had arrived and come to their rescue.

"Proton guns are all well and good," she said. "But sometimes you just need a little help from the Swiss Army." She raised her pocket knife.

"Oh, there you are," Holtzmann said as Erin smiled at Abby.

"Couldn't let you have all the fun," Erin replied.

Abby smiled back. "Okay, let's go save this city and get our receptionist back."

Kevin/Rowan was perched on the ledge of the Mercado. He saw that the Ghostbusters were on their way.

"Here they come," he said out loud. "Let's give them a proper New York welcome, shall we?"

Red clouds swirled above the building. The soldiers and army stood frozen on the sidewalk and in the street.

Kevin/Rowan appeared on the screens all around Times Square.

"Ah, there they are." His tone was mocking. "The Ghostbusters. All dressed up and nowhere to bust. I'll tell you what. I can help you out. Oh, and nice *not* knowing you."

The buildings and modern electronic billboards began to melt away, revealing Times Square of the past. The scariest ghosts of the 1970s were all gathered there, ready to attack.

"I've never been good in a fight," Erin admitted.

"Well, you'd better get good at it." Abby adjusted her pack. "Power up!"

The Ghostbusters switched on their proton packs just as the ghost army rushed at them. The Ghostbusters did what they could to hold them back. They shot proton streams in every direction, throwing ghosts into other ghosts and knocking them around.

A ghost rushed at Abby as she held off another ghost with her beam. She used the proton wand to smash the rushing ghost in the face, an explosion of ectoplasm bursting out of him.

Patty threw proton grenades, sending several ghosts flying in another explosion of ectoplasm.

117

Holtzmann hit a trigger on her proton pack. Two smaller proton pistols popped out. She began firing with dual-hand precision. At Patty's look, she said, "Just a little bonus I gave myself. I'll whip you up a set if we manage to not die right now."

That seemed fair. Patty blew a ghost backward like a bowling ball into other ghosts. They scattered. It seemed like the ghosts were becoming afraid of the Ghostbusters.

"All right!" Abby said. "Anybody else want a piece of this? Bring it on!"

"Okay, amp it down, tiger," Erin told her. "Miles to go."

Abby nodded and then headed off, looking tough and mighty, toward the entryway to the Mercado. The ghosts moved aside to let Erin, Holtzmann, and Patty through. The first battle had been won.

The Ghostbusters walked through the lines of cops and the National Guard, who were now disco statues.

"Seems odd," Abby remarked. Then it got weirder as Slimer, the ghost driver, sped past them in Ecto-1. A lot of other ghosts were piled into the car, singing and yelling like it was a party.

"Well, at least somebody's having a good time," Abby said as the car sped away.

The doors to the Mercado building were locked. Erin noticed a glowing crack in the ground that originated from the basement.

"All right." Abby raised her wand. "Stay back." She was about to blow open the doors, when they opened by themselves. The Ghostbusters entered cautiously.

The lobby was covered with ectoplasm. In the center was a huge swirling whirlpool of energy.

"All right," Abby said. "Let's get down to the basement. We'll start by turning off his little science experiment."

They were about to go downstairs when a huge piano slid out and blocked their way.

Kevin/Rowan appeared on a balcony. He wasn't wearing a shirt, and his chest glowed. He was pale, with sleepless circles under his eyes, which made him extra creepy.

"Kevin?" Abby asked.

"Is that what this thing's name is?" Rowan's voice boomed from inside the body. "He seemed more like a Chet to me." He looked at the Ghostbusters. "I see there's five of you now."

Abby and Erin looked at each other. Then they realized he was counting a confused tenant from the building who was standing next to them.

"Who are you?" Erin asked.

"I was napping. I just came down to get my mail."

Erin was nice about pointing the way out, while Abby shouted, "Get out of here!"

Screaming, the tenant fled out the front door.

Patty shrugged. "Probably should've given him a heads up as to what's out there."

"Well, you've had a long journey," Kevin/Rowan told the Ghostbusters. "You look winded. Have a seat." Chairs slid up behind them.

Holtzmann sat down, but the chair slid away from her just before she made contact. She fell to the floor. Kevin/Rowan chuckled.

"I appreciate the joke," Holtzmann said. "It's a classic."

"I have to compliment you," Kevin/Rowan told them. "I am surprised you made it this far. You're intelligent, courageous, and I'm impressed. I'm willing to let you remain as my companions."

"And I'm willing to beat you up," Abby said with a snort.

"I saw your grandmother on the other side," Kevin/Rowan told her. "I kicked her in the face."

Abby wasn't shaken. "Yeah, listen, I know you're real cozy in the form of Kevin, but time to hop out. We like him," she said.

"Yeah, he just started figuring out the phones!" Holtzmann added.

"As you wish," Rowan told her. He left Kevin's body limp at the top of the balcony. The body started to fall over.

The Ghostbusters rushed to Kevin and managed to protect him.

In a chilling voice, Rowan asked, "What form would you prefer I take?"

"Nothing fancy. Just keep it simple," Holtzmann suggested.

Patty had an idea. "I'll tell you what I prefer. A nice little friendly ghost. Like in a sheet."

"Oh?" Rowan smiled as he morphed into a white-sheet cartoon ghost. It did seem happy.

"Is this what you want? Adorable clip art?" Rowan asked.

Patty nodded. "Yes. I have no problem with that. Thank you."

Ghostly Rowan's smile remained, but his face began to look sinister.

"I don't know. That looks a little murder-y to me," Erin said, taking a step back.

"It is starting to feel different," Abby noted.

"This works for me." Rowan began to grow bigger and even more frightening.

"All right, I didn't know this was going to be a development." Patty backed away.

The ghost grew bigger and bigger and bigger.

"This isn't good," Abby said.

And just then, ghost Rowan raised his hands, creating a giant burst of energy that blew them off their feet and through the Mercado doors.

CHAPTER 16

The Ghostbusters crashed through the front line of agents and cops. The whole platoon went down at once.

"Strike!" Rowan's laughter was eclipsed by an intense—and growing—rumbling sound.

The Ghostbusters looked up just in time to see all the windows blow out of the Mercado as furniture and debris flew out of each floor. Then the whole building began to shake. Giant Rowan, still looking like a ghost cartoon, burst out of the debris. He stared down at the Ghostbusters and roared.

"Run!" Erin shouted.

They jumped up and fled as the beast chased them. Erin was firing her proton pack and running backward.

She hit him in the side. He screamed in pain.

The Ghostbusters used the distraction to turn a corner into an alley. They ducked next to a Dumpster.

"My man was taking some real creative liberties with what we agreed upon." Patty backed up against the wall, trying to hide. He was supposed to look like a cute ghost in a sheet like a kid on Halloween.

Ghost Rowan limped past them, clearly injured. His foot crushed a car as he searched for them.

"See, that's just off-brand," Patty said as Rowan moved farther away.

"What do we do now?" Erin asked with panic in her voice.

"We need to get back there and fire into the portal with more power," Abby said. "If we can do that, then it could cause a reverse reaction." She glanced out from behind the Dumpster. Rowan was gone. For now. . . .

"More power?" Erin asked. "Do we not have our packs set to max now? Because it does feel like this would be the time for that!"

"We're at max," Holtzmann confirmed. "Rowan's got everything too energized, which is why I suggest the following. Now, it's a little risky. It's called 'crossing the streams.'"

Erin's eyes widened. "The thing that was so powerful

our atoms could implode? That's 'a little risky'?"

Patty peeked around the corner. Ghost Rowan was down the street, looking for them with his head spinning, like a freaky owl.

"I mean, he's really just doing his own thing now," Patty said, biting her lower lip.

Abby took a good look at Rowan, then said, "Holtz is right. If successful, it could cause a reverse reaction that would pull any ionized ecto-matter back into its dimension of origin."

"And if it's not successful, then this is most likely not only a suicide mission, but one that involves the most painful death conceivable of all time." Erin rubbed her temples. This wasn't good.

"That's definitely a down side," Abby agreed.

Erin sighed. "Well, we don't have much of a choice, do we?"

The Ghostbusters hurried back to the front of the building. Because of the destruction, the lobby floor had disappeared, exposing the supernatural portal in the basement. Erin was moving so fast, she almost fell into it. Holtzmann grabbed the back of her shirt and pulled her back.

"Okay, fire them up!" Abby said when they were ready.

Erin nodded to Holtzmann. They joined Patty and Abby firing at the portal.

Over her shoulder, Erin saw ghost Rowan.

"He's coming! Cross them up!" Erin shouted as he got closer.

The Ghostbusters entangled their beams, which grew into one massive beam as the portal lit up.

"The portal's too strong. We still don't have enough power to reverse it," Abby told them.

"How do we get more?" Erin was feeling desperate.

Holtzmann had the solution. "We need to one-eighty the polarity with a high concentration electron blast. We just need my negative-charge containment canisters."

"Where are they?" Patty asked, and at the same time Slimer rolled around the corner, still driving Ecto-1. There were happy ghosts hanging off the sides of the car.

Holtzmann looked at the Ecto-1, then answered Patty, "On top of our car."

The Ecto-1 sped toward them and swerved to avoid the portal.

Abby thought fast.

"Let's narrow the target," Abby said with a smile. She pointed at two street lamps nearby. They took aim at the base of the lamps, which exploded, falling across the road

with a slam.

Slimer wasn't paying attention when the lamps fell. He noticed that the road was blocked but it was too late. He turned the wheel and hit the brakes, but the Ecto-1 went up the edge of the sidewalk and flew straight into the portal!

"Aim for the silver canisters!" Holtzmann called out.

The Ghostbusters blasted their beams into the canisters on the roof as the Ecto-1 plummeted. A huge blast exploded out of the portal, sending the Ghostbusters backward. The portal stopped spinning for an instant, changed color, and then it started up again, only this time spinning in reverse.

The ground rumbled. A massive wind blew strong and hard as the portal began sucking everything supernatural into it.

"It's working!" Erin cheered.

Ghost Rowan hung onto the side of a building, while all around them ghosts were being sucked down and away.

A creepy clown ghost zoomed by.

Patty wrinkled her nose. "Glad we didn't have to deal with that one—"

The clown tried to grab Patty as it flew past. "Aaahhh!" She dodged in time, and it was sucked down with the others.

Ghost Rowan was still holding on, fighting the force.

127

"He's too strong," Erin said, voice echoing in the wind. "We can't let the portal close with him still here!"

"I'll get him in!" Abby declared.

"What are you talking about?" Erin asked.

"I'll get him to chase me into it. Keep firing and hold it open," Abby said.

"That's crazy," Erin told her. "How would you make it back?"

Abby ran over and grabbed a cable on the front of a tipped-over fire truck. "This thing runs pretty long."

"That's insane." Erin tried to stop her. "You can't expect that to work!"

"I gotta try," Abby said firmly.

"Abby, no—"

"Erin, I don't know if you've noticed, but I haven't done much else besides this. I've been wondering what's on the other side my whole life. And now I can take a peek!" She tied an end of the cable around her waist. "I'm gonna come back. You just gotta pull the rope. Okay?"

Erin studied Abby's face. "Listen, I—"

Abby stopped her. "Hey. No need to even say it. I am so glad you came back." Abby gave Erin a reassuring smile, then walked out to the center of the street as Erin, Holtzmann, and Patty started firing into the portal to hold it open. "All

right, let's go. Once I'm in there, you just pull me out."

Abby caught ghost Rowan's eye and waved at him. "Yeah, you. You dumb ghost." He turned to her, and she continued to insult him. "Look at yourself! You look ridiculous running around here. You don't seem very powerful!" She zapped him a little with her proton pack.

He growled and limped toward her.

"Yeah, you don't like that, do you?" Abby zapped him a little again. He growled more. Then she fired everything she had at him.

"Okay, I have his attention—" Abby began running away. He came after her, picking up speed. They were almost at the portal when the cable pulled taut. Abby was stuck.

"Oh no." Erin realized the cable was caught under the fallen light pole. "Hold on!" She ran to the car. "I'll get it loose."

"There's no time," said Abby. Rowan was only a few feet away from her.

Abby untied the cable from her body.

"No, wait!" Erin shouted, but Abby leaped into the portal just as Erin freed the cable.

Rowan dove in after her.

They were both gone.

CHAPTER 17

Patty, Holtzmann, and Erin stood sadly, watching the portal close. Erin took a step forward, at a loss for words.

Suddenly, Erin grabbed the cable. She tied it around her waist and jumped into the portal an instant before it closed.

"Erin!" Patty shrieked.

There was a final flash of light that knocked Holtzmann and Patty off their feet. The dark clouds disappeared. The sun rose warm and bright in the sky.

Patty and Holtzmann couldn't believe what had happened. It couldn't be over. The sealed portal still smoked before them. They stared at it, unwilling to accept that this was how it was going to end.

Erin and Abby . . . They couldn't be gone forever. But there was no sign of the portal opening again.

Just as Patty and Holtzmann were about to give up hope, they heard a mighty *SHOOMP!* come from where the portal had been. Abby and Erin shot up out of it! They crashed to the ground, covered in ectoplasm. When Holtzmann and Patty reached them, they were bewildered. . . .

"Oh!" Patty said, noting that both of them now had ghostly white hair.

"What did I just see?" Abby turned to Erin, who just asked, "What year is it?"

Holtzmann couldn't help herself. "2040. Welcome back."

"We did it?" Abby looked around and saw that Holtzmann was grinning.

"You did it," Holtzmann said.

"We *all* did it," Erin said, bringing everyone in for a big hug.

Just then, Kevin joined them. "That's right. We all did it."

They looked over at Kevin.

"All right," Erin said, not quite getting what he meant. "We didn't *all* do it. What did you do?"

"A *lot*, actually. I'll have you know I went over to that power box, pushed a few buttons, then everything got sucked up into the portal and it closed."

"That had nothing to do with anything," Erin protested.

Abby was more encouraging. "No, that may have helped. Good for you, Kevin."

"It did not help," Erin argued. She noticed a stain on his shirt. "And at what point did you get a sandwich?"

Kevin brought a half eaten sub from behind his back. "I was looking for you, and I looked in that deli over there. Listen, let's not turn on each other now. That's not what Ghostbusters are about."

"He has a good point . . . ," Abby said.

Television news began reporting from the scene.

"In the aftermath, still trying to understand what happened—" a reporter was saying.

"—the government trying to claim the event wasn't supernatural—" another said.

In Times Square, a reporter was interviewing a man on the street. "I'm telling you. I did not evacuate. I got into a cab being driven by a skeleton. Don't tell me that was no science experiment gone wrong."

Mayor Bradley was also being interviewed. The reporter asked, "You're honestly going to sit here and tell me that we didn't see ghosts?"

 132

"Yes. Wait. What?" the mayor was confused.

For another channel, a reporter said, "Homeland Security is claiming it was an experiment gone wrong."

"The Ghostbusters have been quiet about taking credit . . . ," a reporter was saying when a woman interrupted, "Oh, it was the Ghostbusters. I saw them. It was amazing."

Later that night, the Ghostbusters went out to celebrate. Erin sat with Patty, Holtzmann, and Abby. Erin and Abby had tried dying their hair back, but it just looked odd.

Abby looked for a waitress. "Saved New York and we still can't get someone to serve us."

"I'd like to make a toast." Holtzmann raised her drink.

Erin rolled her eyes. "Oh, here we go."

"When I met Abby, I was so happy finally to have my first real friend. And now with all of you, I have my first real family. I truly love you guys." Holtzmann sat down.

"Wow, that was like a real thing," Patty said.

They glanced up to find Jennifer Lynch approaching.

"What did I tell you?" Jennifer Lynch said. "People always move on. We want to thank you for your discretion. It's not working at all, but thank you."

"It's better to keep a low profile. Who cares about credit?

133

Let's just focus on the important stuff," Erin told her.

Abby smiled at Erin.

"I'm sorry we can't give you any kind of formal recognition," Jennifer went on. "But please know that what you did was phenomenal."

"We appreciate that," Patty said.

Jennifer had one more thing to say. "Mayor Bradley also sends his thanks. He couldn't voice that out loud, but he said it with his eyes."

"Tell him I said . . . ," Holtzmann began.

Jennifer cut her off. She whispered, "We'd like you to continue studying this subject. We need to be better prepared. Just in case. Whatever you need to keep you going." Her voice got even softer. "Anything at all."

"Anything at all?" Holtzmann echoed. There was a twinkle in her eyes.

CHAPTER 18

Erin, Abby, Holtzmann, and Patty stood across the street from a fancy firehouse. It was the perfect place for a new Ghostbusters headquarters. They exchanged pleased looks.

"Oh yes," Patty said, eyes roaming from the sidewalk to the top of the roof.

"I claim the upstairs," Holtzmann declared.

"You can't claim an entire floor!" Patty argued.

"Just did!" Holtzmann was ready to fight for it.

Erin and Abby looked at each other with massive grins.

"Not bad, ghost girl," Abby said.

"Thank you. I will proudly take that title." Erin was beaming.

Erin and Abby tried the Abby-and-Holtzmann elaborate handshake. It was a disaster.

"We'll get our own," Abby assured her.

Then a black hearse with a red roof slowly rolled up to the firehouse.

"Oh no. Is that . . . ?" Erin said.

"Patty's uncle," Abby finished.

Patty's uncle got out of the hearse. "Where is it?" he asked, wanting to know what had happened to the hearse he had let his niece borrow.

Patty faced him. "I already told you!"

"I don't want to hear that my hearse is in another dimension!" He put his hands on his hips.

"Look, if I could cross over and get it for you, I would!" Patty met his gaze.

"Let's let them work this out," Abby suggested as she and Erin followed Holtzmann into the firehouse, leaving Patty and her uncle on the street.

Two weeks later they were all settled into their new headquarters. Abby stood at the door, paying the Chinese food delivery guy. She opened the carton to find it stuffed with wontons. There were too many to even count.

"I know what you did," he told her.

"All right, don't get weird on me," Abby said.

"You're very brave," the deliveryman said.

"All I want is a healthy ratio of wontons to broth, not this madness. This is just a science laboratory. Keep it cool." Abby closed the door and walked over to Erin, who was busy opening up a box. "The new book?!" she asked.

"It's here." Erin pulled out a copy of their brand new book. On the back cover was a new embarrassing photo of Erin and Abby in black turtlenecks.

Abby read the cover. *"A Glimpse into the Unknown."*

"Oh, did we go with the shorter title?" Erin asked. "I thought . . ."

Abby held up the book where the full title was printed. *"A Journey into a Portal; Catching Sight of the Other Dimension: Discovering the Undiscoverable: A Curiosity Piqued and Peaked."* She ran a loving finger over the cover. "I still think we should've gone with *There and Back Again, A Scientist's Tale.*"

"Next time," Erin assured her.

The phone rang. Kevin answered it. "Ghostbusters. Please give a detailed description of your apparition."

Abby gave Kevin the thumbs-up.

"Well, we've got a lot to do," Erin said as she and Abby reached Holtzmann, who was working with some new gadgets.

"Speaking of which, how we doing over here?" Erin asked her.

"I am working on some next level stuff," Holtzmann said. "Real outside the box, like put me back in the box because I am scared of what I'm doing sort of stuff."

Abby checked out the large containment unit. "This thing running?"

"Quite smoothly." Holtzmann tapped the side. "I would say don't be in a room with it for longer than an hour at any one time."

"Well, I think we can probably aim higher—" Erin noticed a woman studying some wires behind the unit. "Oh, I'm sorry, I didn't see anyone there."

"You haven't met?" said Holtzmann. "This is my mentor, Elizabeth Gorin."

"Oh, it's so nice to finally meet—" Erin was cut off.

"This is reckless, Jillian," Dr. Gorin scolded. "You're breeding fissile plutonium with insufficient criticality moderation. All someone has to do is sneeze too hard and everyone in this building is disintegrated. Do you know how powerful that is?"

"I was bad," Holtzmann said, head down.

**138**

"And I've never been more proud of you," Dr. Gorin brought Holtzmann in for a hug. "Now let's make this more powerful, shall we?" She started turning knobs.

"Yeah!" Holtzmann got back to work.

Erin walked away, a little concerned. "Power within reason," she told Holtzmann.

"But don't limit yourselves," Abby added.

"Definitely not," Erin clarified. "But at the same time, imagine a 'responsible cap.'"

Patty came running down the stairs. "Hey, you gotta check this out! Come up to the roof!"

The Ghostbusters gathered on the rooftop. Patty pointed to the distance.

"I guess it's a thank-you from New York," Patty said.

"That's very thoughtful of them," Holtzmann grinned.

The Empire State Building was all lit up—with the Ghostbusters logo on the side.

"Well, that's not terrible," Abby said proudly.

"No it's not. Not terrible at all," Erin agreed.